SOMEDAY

A Novella

CORINNA TURNER

unSeen

Lyrics from 'Where Are You Bound' by John Glynn. Used by Permission.

'Lami, Maria and Hajara' by '100 Women' programme, first published as 'Escaping
Boko Haram' on the *BBC* website on 27th October 2014. Used by Permission.

'Baba Goni' by Barbara Jones, first published as 'Defiled and Bloody' in *The Mail
on Sunday* on 18th May 2014. Used by Permission.

'Chibok Girls Who Walked to Freedom' by Ruth Maclean, first published in *The
Times* on 12th October 2014. Used by Permission.

'Ladi Apagu' by Chika Oduah. Used by Permission.

Cover design by Corinna Turner and Regina Doman.

A catalogue record for this book is available from the British Library.

ISBN: 978-1-910806-02-9 (paperback)
Also available as an eBook

* Zephyr Publishing, UK—Corinna Turner, T/A

Thanks must also go to the generous developers of these beautiful Open Source fonts: Source
Sans Pro, IMPACT LABEL REVERSED, Rosario, Roboto and CAPTURE IT 1 & 2
And to: www.all-silhouettes.com

CONTENTS

FOREWORD

The heart of Nigeria was wounded when 276 schoolgirls were kidnapped from a school by extremist group Boko Haram on 15th April 2014. A number of the girls escaped shortly afterwards, but two years on, the others have not been found. Rumours have abounded: the girls have been killed, they have been married off, they are being held in underground bunkers. But the truth is that their fate is known only to themselves, their captors, and to God.

The tragedy is that these girls only represent a small proportion of the total number of women being kept captive—there are more than 1,000 still being held. Kidnappings are continually ongoing. Both men and women are taken. Those kidnapped face forced conversion and for women, forced marriage. Many of those they abduct are forced to fight.

In north-eastern Nigeria especially, Christians have been targeted simply because of their faith, and some of them have faced the choice of their faith or their life. When they initially thought that they were the target of unfair and brutal attacks leading to multiple deaths and the destruction of Churches, the extremists raised the level of their insensitivity, inhumanity and brutality by attacking anyone who refused to share in their warped philosophy of life. Hence, even moderate and dialogue-loving Muslims like their Christian neighbours have suffered killings and the destruction of places of worship and property. Millions have been internally displaced and many others are languishing as refugees in neighbouring countries. Some Christians who have managed to return to what were once their homes have found their farms in ruins, while hunger, disease and homelessness stare them uncharitably in the face!

I hope that reading SOMEDAY will help people living in a different culture, in a security most Christians, and indeed Muslims, in north-eastern Nigeria can scarcely imagine, to better understand what people are suffering here. I hope it will also help Christians to understand how precious their faith is and bring them into a closer relationship with our Lord Jesus Christ. I am delighted that the proceeds from the sale of this novella will be going to Aid to the Church in Need, a charity which provides the Church in Nigeria with a great deal of support, and has stood in solidarity with us in our time of need.

+ *Ignatius A. Kaigama,*
Archbishop of Jos, Nigeria.

February 2016

INTRODUCTION

In 2014 Boko Haram, an organization of Muslim militants and fundamentalists, kidnapped 276 schoolgirls in Nigeria. Despite extensive searches they have never been found but a number did get away in the course of the abduction to report rape and torture and murder.

This book sets a similar action in the UK at a girl's boarding school. The victims are of mixed religious persuasion including a Muslim and a Japanese Shintoist while some do not believe at all but the quandaries they face are those that have been faced in any period of oppression throughout history. Is open defiance the only moral option? Or is it better to seem to go along with those in control, in reality watching and waiting for an opportunity to escape or at least be alive to denounce them when the reign of terror ends? Martyrdom or surrender?

Such decisions pre-occupied those faced with Nazism in Germany in the first half of the last century and those faced with communism in Russia in the second half. Today such dilemmas confront those coerced by *Jihadists*. What makes this examination different is the vulnerability and age of the girls who have nothing but hope, faith and courage on which to survive and the belief that someday it will be all over. Someday they will be free.

Sustained by faith, plagued by doubt, living in daily fear they deal with the situation both as a group and as individuals and the dynamics of the whole are determined by the dictates of lone consciences. As Ruth, for example, finds it impossible to deny Christ, her terrified friends, not wanting her to die regardless of whether they believe or not, scream at her to give in. I suspect readers will be divided too.

Although the author has placed the mass kidnap in Britain rather than Africa—which makes it easy to follow events without having first to acclimatize to a different geographical and social background—the story follows much of the real one in the numbers and escapes. Placing the abduction on British soil also hugely increases the shock value as the reader cannot escape asking *could this happen here?*

Of course the kidnappers do not keep their victims here and there is only a limited period for any search to be successful. That is a necessary device because in a small, heavily populated island, the inhabitants of which are not in sympathy with Islam, the challenge of tracking down the perpetrators would be comparatively easy as against the vastness and remoteness of Muslim Albania—where despite its history of moderate Islam, extremism has gained a foothold in recent years. It also hugely increases the dramatic tension.

The book introduces us not only to the victims but to those involved in the story at the fringes including the soldiers and cadets who join the hunt. Two are Muslim brothers with a sister already being turned towards extremism; and normal, pleasant parents who are helpless in the face of it.

Others merely watch the story unfold through the safety of their television or phone screens. Time passes and other news headlines take over until the story fades from national consciousness but some are determined never to forget.

Christians are persecuted the world over as also are those of many minority faiths. Many face serious threats to life and limb in places such as Syria. Others must choose between livelihood and conscience as in Britain and between those two very different examples lies a vast range of intimidation and pressure to conform.

One of the greatest threats is Islam extremism because it uses force on a very large and brutal scale as the crucifixions, beheadings and burning alive of Daesh illustrate. As this book demonstrates, that can make life unpleasant for ordinary Muslims who want nothing more than to get on with their lives and with their neighbours.

Aid to the Church in Need is an organization which brings much-needed moral and financial support to Christians persecuted throughout the world and I have the honour to serve as its Special Envoy for Religious Freedom. The kidnapping of the Nigerian girls should never be written off merely as an unpleasant historical event, about which we can no longer do anything and I am grateful to Corinna Turner for keeping alive the memory and reminding us of the shocking reality of the victims' situation.

On a daily basis extreme Islam creates many more victims: the young who have their heads turned towards *Jihadism*; the girls who imagine they please God by becoming the brides of men they have never met and the heartbroken families who find out too late that they have gone; women who do not wish to view the world through an inch-wide slit in a *bhurka*; those who convert to other religions; frantic parents who suspect their children are being radicalized.

This book leaves you wanting to know more, wanting the girls to be rescued, wanting a happy ending. Alas, real life is different.

*Ann **Widdecombe,** January 2016*

Words are more than sounds,
Falling off an empty tongue.

John Glynn, 'Where Are You Bound'

RUTH

What the...! I jerk awake, ears ringing, heart pounding in my chest...

Oh, the fire alarm.

I'm closest to the door, so I swing my legs out of bed and find my way to the light switch. Gemma groans loudly as light floods the dorm, and retreats into her duvet, so only a few tufts of short red hair show. Annabel is already pushing long blond hair back from her face and groping sleepily for her dressing gown but Yoko sits up straight in bed, wide-eyed.

"It's just the fire alarm," I shout over the racket, pointing to the door. "We have to go outside."

Yoko looks slightly reassured—she hasn't understood everything I said, but she's figured it out. I pull on my dressing gown and shoes, pointing at them and smiling encouragingly at her—no time to look it up in her Japanese dictionary—she does the same.

"Gemma?" yawns Annabel, grabbing a hair tie. "D'you want to burn to death?"

"It's just a practice," grumbles Gemma, but she finally pushes back her duvet and sits up.

I beckon to Yoko and head out the door. Annabel follows.

"Oh, wait for me, why don't you?" Gemma shouts.

I carry on along the corridor. She'll catch us up. It's not a practice and she knows it. Sure enough, she's already hopping along after us from one foot to the other, as she puts her shoes on.

There's no crush on the central stairs—we're the only year in the main school tonight and the sixth form have a separate block. There's still a subdued murmur of complaint filling the air. It would have to happen tonight, wouldn't it?

"See," says Gemma snidely, catching me all the way up, "if there was a God, He wouldn't make this happen before our Physics exam, would He? Or did you not say enough prayers?"

"Here we go again," says Annabel, pushing her mass of blond hair back and readying her hair tie. "Obsessed, much?"

1

I tuck my slightly shorter dark brown hair behind my ears and say nothing. Am I the only one who can see that Gemma's parents have spent too long on mission and not enough time with her? She wouldn't be so jealous of God if she wasn't hurting so much.

GEMMA

I open my mouth to reply to Annabel... break off, eyes widening at the sight of a uniformed—armed!—soldier rushing up the stairwell.

"Outside!" he yells, with some sort of inner-city accent. "Hurry up, everyone out!"

"Is there actually a fire?" gasps Annabel, her ridiculously long hair tumbling all around her again as she almost drops her hair tie. "Not just mice chewing wires again..."

But Ruth frowns slightly as she looks at the soldier—yeah, he's not a fireman.

He sees our expressions. "There's been a bomb threat. *Out,* now! Where is everyone else?"

"There isn't anyone else," Annabel says over her shoulder, taking off down the stairs as though... she's just heard there might be a bomb in the building.

The soldier looks annoyed—yells after her, "Where are the younger ones?"

"Year seven are at an adventure training camp," I reply, but I start down the stairs as well. Bomb threats are usually hoaxes but I'm so not risking it. Not the way things are at the moment. "Year eight, IT camp; year nine, French exchange; year ten, Venice, English trip. It's just us and the sixth form."

The soldier swears loudly and starts herding us back down the stairs, giving me a push to hurry me along.

"Hey!" I protest. "If I fall and break something and you have to carry me, it's going to take even longer, isn't it?"

Ruth shoots the man another looks and trots on down the stairs, guiding Yoko with her, like she's more scared of the soldier than of the bomb. And though I'd never admit it, I do kind of respect her opinion—at least on anything that doesn't concern the divine Sky Fairy.

The man's scruffier than any soldier I've ever seen—and since when do they dispatch armed men to evacuate civilians?

ALLELUIA

"Quit shoving, would you?" I snap at the man who's chivvying us towards the assembly point. "Think I wanna stay in there with a bomb, huh?"

"Hurry up," he says.

That's all he's said since he met us outside the sixth form block and I'm sick of it. "Jesus loves you too," I tell him.

He smacks me across the head and I gasp in pain. For a moment I can only gape at him. Did this soldier seriously just hit me? Then I see the assembly point ahead and it evaporates from my mind.

There's a row of trucks and a couple of horse vans—horseboxes, they call them over here—pulled up in the parking lot and more soldiers are forcing girls into them at gunpoint. Everyone looks scared—a few girls are crying. *Lord, what is going on?*

"Show us some ID!" Miss Trott is yelling. She's the senior housemistress. "You are not taking these girls unless we see some ID! Where are the police? Where's bomb disposal?" She grabs a soldier's arm, "ID, *now!*"

The soldier un-shoulders his rifle and casually smashes the butt into Miss Trott's face. She crumples to the ground in a horrible, boneless way. I jerk in a shocked breath—then grab Jill and Karen. "*Run!*"

I shove them towards the wood and dive at the soldier who hit me—after a moment of confusion I'm rewarded by the sound of running footsteps on the gravel path. The soldier shoves me away so hard I fall, tearing pyjamas and knee. *Ow...* Blood oozes brightly across my black skin. But Jill and Karen have disappeared into the dark.

The soldier swings back to me—my heart freezes in my

3

throat, everything freezes as he brings up the rifle and cocks it, hate filling his angry eyes...

ANNABEL

I can't believe what I'm seeing. A soldier just attacked Miss Trott. And another is about to shoot Alleluia Williams, the charismatic (oh my, in every sense) head of the Christian Union. What sort of soldiers *are* these?

"*No shooting!*" The guy who hit Miss Trott is yelling it. "NO shooting, remember? Hurry up, get them over here..."

"Two of them ran..."

"Leave them, hurry up. Where are the rest?"

He's shouting that at me... no, at the soldier behind us, who's... whoa! He's dragging Gemma by the arm and Ruth by her dark hair! They must've tried to bolt. These aren't real soldiers, are they... Why am I always so slow on the uptake?

"This is all of them. The others are away on trips."

Cursing from the... officer? Leader? "Fill up three trucks," he yells. "Leave the others."

They're shoving Ally up into a horsebox, un-shot, thank God. Miss Trott isn't moving, but they won't let the rest of the house staff help her.

"The young ones would have been worth more," the leader is grumbling. "Who knows if this lot are virgins?"

Did he really just say that?

Yoko's beginning to sniff quietly. Ruth's still being dragged, so pushing aside my hair, which I still haven't managed to do anything with, I put an awkward arm around her.

"Get in," orders another man, as we reach a white truck that looks like it should be out delivering washing machines or furniture. I head towards it at once with Yoko, then realize Ruth and Gemma haven't moved.

"If you want to die, sit down here," says the man harshly, "We will kill you. If you don't want to die, you will enter the truck."

RUTH

No shooting. So should we make another run for it?

The guy can tell what we're thinking, because he pulls out a wicked knife, smirks as though he'd quite like us to try it, and says, *"In"*.

Maybe not. Gemma still seems a bit shaken from being slammed into the wall when he caught us, so I help her climb up.

"Get in," I can hear the man by the next truck saying. "Don't worry, we won't touch you."

I move to scramble in after Gemma, but for a moment the soldier presses me against the back of the truck, his hand feeling my bum. Then he puts it between my legs. I can't move, I can't think what to do. I want to scream and try to get away, but I'm afraid that might trigger something even worse... Then the man shoves me up into the truck... and his hand is gone—but my heart pounds in my throat and terror washes through me and it feels like I understand for the first time that this is bad, this is *really bad...*

"We are *al-Qabda*," the leader is shouting, marching up and down in front of the trucks, brandishing the weapon he can't fire right now. "We will purify the world of infidels. There will be no more sinful education. Now you will study Islam and learn to please your husbands. Nothing more! *Allahu akbar!*"

"*Allahu akbar!*" roar the others. One of the house staff faints.

The leader glances at them dismissively. "Those ones are too old. No man will want them. Let's go!"

The roll-back is pulled down and locked, plunging us into darkness. I sit down beside Gemma and try not to shake, but now that my body's started it can't stop. That one touch makes me feel... *violated.* If only I'd grabbed my Bible, or my rosary or *anything*... Actually, it may not be very safe to have things like that, just now.

I make do with crossing myself and clasping my hands

tightly together and trying to form some prayer a little more articulate than a simple scream of, 'help us!' But I can't.

Help us. Help us, Lord. Help us.

DANIYAH

The man is reaching for the truck door... my mouth is so dry I'm not sure I can speak, but this is my last chance.

"Please..." I croak, "*Allahu akbar!* I'm Muslim. Please let me out!"

"Muslim, *you?*" The way his eyes rove over my hair makes me feel like I'm naked. "In this school of infidels?"

"I don't go to any of the Christian services," I say in a rush, desperate to get it out, "I leave lessons to pray if necessary..."

"If you're a good Muslim girl, you'll be glad of the chance to be the bride of a brave *Jihadi.* You'll have an honourable marriage, you've no need to be afraid... *if* you're telling the truth."

He slams one door and reaches for the other.

"But... my family..."

"Not as good Muslims as *you* claim to be, or they wouldn't have sent you here, would they?"

"But..."

The door slams in my face. The engine starts. I sink down on the floor and wrap my arms around my head. It's dark in here, too dark to see, but I'm still afraid to look at anyone else, like they'll hate me for trying to escape.

They sent me here instead of a secular school because they are *good Muslims.* The thought pounds through my head. *Because they thought at a Christian school I would be taught modest behaviour and wouldn't hang around with boys. I was going to be a human rights lawyer. Going to help people. And now...*

I raise my hands and try to make *dua.* But the words won't come.

Allah... Allah... Allah... help us...

6

ALLELUIA

They slam the ramp up, the engine starts—the horse van begins to move. My heart's still beating so hard it's physically painful and I can't see anything but the muzzle of that gun, pointing straight into my face... I'm afraid I'm about to start screaming and never stop.

No. The Lord has preserved my life. I've gotta get hold of myself.

I drag myself to my feet, ignoring the ache from my bleeding knee, and try to get a look through the high window. There's a strange orange glow in the sky... Grabbing the window edge, I pull myself up and look out. Black smoke fills the sky and flames are licking from the main school building. They set the school on *fire?*

For a second the horse van's tail lights illuminate the sign behind us as we turn onto the main road.

Chisbrook Hall Girls School
A Methodist Foundation Welcoming All
Age 11-18, Boarding and Day

Most of us love our school, but right now even I'm wishing Mom and Dad had sent me somewhere else.

Why us? Why us, Lord?

How can this be happening here, in the UK? I thought it was Mom and Dad this could happen to, out on mission. Or back home in the US, where it seems like people wander into schools with guns all the time.

Not us, *here...*

GEMMA

Ruth's sitting beside me, shaking so hard I know I missed something. 'Cause Ruth's the last person I'd expect to freak out. But when I grope for her hands in the dark I find them clasped. She's praying. The familiar anger surges through me and I try to

7

yank them apart. "There's no God! We're being kidnapped by bloody religious maniacs and you still think there's a God! I don't believe you! How can you be so smart most of the time and so thick about this?"

Ruth doesn't say anything. Doesn't mean she's totally lost it. She's not exactly Miss Talkative.

"I often wonder the same about you," says Annabel from nearby, sounding almost normal.

"Oh, shut up," I snarl. "You think God's watching over us, do you?"

"I certainly hope He is, given the circumstances."

I almost laugh, but I'm too angry. "You're mad. And you'd better watch what you say around these men or they'll kill you."

"They're supposed to treat 'People of the Book' okay," says Annabel. "I'm sure it says so in the Quran."

"Yeah? Well, I saw them shoving Daniyah from year twelve into another truck, so if you think you're going to get treated better than her, you're going to be disappointed. Anyway, I happen to know it also says in the Quran that they should beat women and chop unbelievers' heads off. So just keep your mouth shut and do whatever they tell you, okay?"

I shove my hands through my short red hair, trying to get my temper under control. After a moment I drop them again and raise my voice. "Hey, is there anyone in here who speaks Japanese?"

Silence. Not exactly silence. Sobbing and sniffling. Well, surely Yoko can figure out that she's got to do as she's told. If she can understand what she's being told...

"It's not that simple, Gemma." Ruth speaks at last. Her voice is almost steady, but I'm still sure something happened while I was feeling dizzy.

"What isn't?"

"Doing what they tell us. The first thing they'll probably tell us to do is recite those words that make you Muslim."

"So we'll recite them. It doesn't make you anything if you do it under duress."

"You think it doesn't? *They'll* certainly regard you as Muslim forevermore."

"They can think what they like, it won't be true."

"Well, I'm not saying them. No Christian should."

Her quiet statement chills me. Surely Ruth, one of the most obliging people I know, isn't going to choose *now* to be difficult? "Maybe they won't want us to."

But I don't even sound like I'm convincing myself.

ALLELUIA

We're on the highway now. My knee is still hurting. I can feel a trickle of blood running down my leg. I can't tell which way we're going. I sit down again and try to take stock. Jill and Karen got away. The house staff were left behind, alive. Miss Trott... hurt but alive, I reckon. I saw them manhandling Ruth, of all people. She must've tried to run.

Reverend Philips says I bring almost as many people to Christian Union with my mouth as I scare away and that's saying something. But Ruth brings just as many without hardly opening her mouth at all, so go figure. Well, it's not her that brings people any more than it's me, of course. It's Jesus our Saviour; so it's not really a mystery.

That militant atheist girl—what's her name, Gemma—the red-headed wildcat who hangs out with Ruth a lot, I wasn't so surprised to see her being dragged around. I hope she keeps her mouth shut. Dad says these wackos hate atheists worse than Christians.

Oh no, what about Deborah? Is she year eleven? No, she's year ten, isn't she? So she's in Venice, praise God. But they brought Daniyah... Why, for pity's sake?

But the point is, they left lots of people behind, so any moment we should hear sirens and get rescued.

We've just gotta be patient, right?

ANNABEL

I've finally managed to tie my hair back. I forgot about it

for... what seemed a long time. I've always been so proud of my long blond hair. Now I wish I didn't have quite so much of it. Those men... they have funny ideas about hair, don't they...?

How long have we been driving? Why haven't the police stopped us yet, or the real army?

"What's taking so long?" I whisper, kind of to myself, but Gemma answers.

"The school was on fire, they could hardly just run in and phone the police!" She raises her voice, slightly. "No one in here has a phone, right? *Please* tell me you'd have mentioned it by now?"

No answer. Our mobiles are locked in the phone cupboard during the week, only allowed out at weekends.

"I thought the fire alarms were connected to the fire station?" I say. Gemma's lucky, her hair is really short...

"I think they are, but the first people on the scene will be firemen, won't they? Then the police. Then they've got to get a description of the vehicles from whichever of the staff are still conscious and making sense."

"Surely one of them memorized a number plate?" a new voice chimes in. A strong local accent...

"Sasha?" I check. One of the day girls from our year. At least there's one more person in here not having hysterics. But her hair is quite long too. Long and frizzy.

"Yeah, it's Sasha. They'll have got the plates, surely? People always get the plates on TV."

"The plates were covered in mud about an inch thick." Ruth delivers this awful news very apologetically.

Ruth's hair is fairly long... "Still... how many trucks are driving around at this time?"

"Rather a lot, I imagine," snaps Gemma. "Didn't you hear the birds? It's near dawn. Every delivery lorry in the UK will be out and about soon. Still, for this... they'll stop every truck in the country if they have to."

"We'll switch vehicles," says Ruth, even more softly than usual—I hardly hear her. "Any time now..."

"Aren't you Miss Cheerful," says Gemma. But from the

shake in her voice, I can tell she thinks Ruth is right.

Someone wriggles past me and starts, from the sound of it, pawing at the bottom of the roll-down door.

"Who's that...? I heard them lock it..." It's my turn to speak apologetically.

"It's me." Ruth's voice. "I'm looking for a panel or something that might be covering wiring. For the lights."

"Yes!" Gemma's hiss is ferocious. She shoves her way past me and begins scrabbling around as well.

"I'm not convinced it's in here with us," Ruth adds quickly. "I think the lights are too low down. But."

But. We're jolly well going to make sure. I've caught on. They want to try and flash SOS to the other traffic—or at least make the lights behave oddly. Like we saw in that film last term.

Someone *might* notice.

ALLELUIA

No one's got a phone and I can't find any wiring anywhere. Every time I touch something and get hopeful it's just another bit of horse equipment. Still... "This is a horse van, not a prison van," I say out loud. "How secure can it be?"

"There's a door up front here," someone calls. Sounds like Becky, from my year. "But it's locked."

"Oh? 'Scuse me..." I start working my way through to the front.

"Becky?" I've reached a doorway.

"Is that you, Ally? I seriously cannot see you *at all*. The door's in here. It's the living area. I thought we might be able to bash them over the head with something, but they've blocked off the opening into the cab. The good thing about it is that they can't see what we're doing."

"Where's the door?"

"Here..." She taps on the wall beside us, her hand a pale blur. She's right, I can't see my own hands at all.

I reach out and feel around. A door. I try the handle. Locked, yeah. But there's a big window next to it, with a board

11

nailed over the middle, cutting out almost all the light. I move that way and bump into... a sink unit?

"I bet we can kick that door in," I say to Becky. "But if not, perhaps we can get out the window."

"We're on the motorway. We'll have to wait until we come off."

"You can bet we'll be changing vehicles really soon. We should go now."

"But they'll have to come off and slow down to change vehicles. We should wait! We must be doing fifty or sixty miles an hour, Ally!"

"It's got to be now! How long will it take us all to jump? If we're on a normal road they can slam the brakes on the moment the first one goes and get out and stop most of the rest. They can't exactly reverse back down the highway to catch us, can they? Well, I guess they could, but they'd attract exactly the attention they need to avoid. I'm going *now*."

Becky's silent for a long moment. "I'm waiting for them to slow down," she says at last. I open my mouth to argue, but... she's probably worried about breaking something, she's a ballerina. Quite a good one. There's no time to argue about it... I pull her back into the horse area and shut the door.

"Listen, everyone," I shout, over the engine and road noise. "We can get out up front so we plan to jump. I think we should go now, because they won't be able to do much about it—and I figure we'll be changing vehicles soon so any delay and we'll miss our chance. Becky's going to wait until we pull off the highway, but seriously, guys, I think you should come with me now."

There's a shocked silence, punctuated by sobs from people who clearly haven't taken in a word I've said.

"Ally, we're on the *motorway!*" Megan says. "You can't be serious! We'll be run over!"

"If we survive the impact!" says Frankie.

"Don't you understand?" I yell, desperate to make them see. "These men are going to force us to become Muslim—or kill us if we refuse. That's what they *do!* Either way, they're

12

going to sell us as sex slaves and we're going to spend every day of the rest of our lives being raped and cooking and cleaning for beasts who think we're nothing but animals made to serve them. *That* is what awaits us if we don't get out of here! We've more chance of escape if we go now! It's worth the risk!"

BECKY

"Anyway," shouts Ally, "We're in the slow lane and the door's on the left. We'll land on the emergency lane. We're not gonna get hit! Who's with me?"

There's a murmur of agreement and some girls push forwards, others stay put.

"You're mad!" says Frankie.

Megan makes a sound of agreement. "The fall will kill you! Or they'll shoot you!"

"Let them!" says Ally. "This is our best chance! I'd rather die than go with them anyway."

Her certainty is infectious. Most of the *compos mentis* girls are now crowding forward, as far as I can tell. Am I doing the right thing? It just seems such an unnecessary risk—one bad break and I might never dance again—everything I've worked for, for so long, gone... But if they see Ally and the others jumping now, will I get a chance once we slow down?

"Come on," says Ally. "Those who're sure they're going to jump, to the front. Don't go up to the door unless you're really going to do it or you'll stop others getting through. Okay?"

Another murmur of agreement from the group around her. My insides are churning with indecision. I crouch down beside one of the sobbers—Jasmin from my year—and try to get her to understand what we're doing, but it's useless.

"Right," Ally's shouting again. "When we kick this door in, we jump at once, straight after the other, we make it quick! Curl in a ball, you'll bounce better. Okay?"

The people at the front sound pretty determined, but... I wriggle through to Ally. "You'd better go first," I whisper in her ear.

"What? I'll go last, make sure they all get out..."

"No, go first, Ally. If the men see the door open, and then someone hesitates... Going first is hardest."

She grabs my hand. "Come *now*, Becky, please... I know the dancing is important to you, but it's not worth..."

I shake my head, though she'll barely see it. I know with absolute certainty that I can't jump from this vehicle, not at this speed. I'm starting to think I should, but I know I won't. "We can't all be as brave as you, Ally. Just go, for God's sake."

Her black face is invisible in the darkness but I know she's scowling 'cause I took the Lord's name in vain. I s'pose I'm just not sure enough of what comes after to throw myself out of a moving vehicle.

She raises her voice and prays unusually succinctly. "Oh Lord, grant us Your protection! In the name of Jesus! Amen!"

Rather more people echo her 'Amen' than would usually do so. This sort of situation does that to people. Ally is already kicking the door. Several people join her and for a few hour-long moments there's just thudding and grunting and... splintering. A rectangle of light as the door flies open... Ally doesn't hesitate. She just yells, *"Praise God!"* and jumps out.

And she's gone.

GEMMA

There's no wiring, and we can't find a weak spot on the sides of the van. We've kicked the roll-down door until our feet are bruised. We can't get out, but... "Praying isn't going to help, Ruth!"

"Have you thought of something else to try?"

"No," I say grudgingly, yanking irritably at my short hair.

"Then praying is the only thing that is going to help."

"He's not *there*. And he's definitely not looking out for..."

There's a squeal of brakes—the van swerves left, then right, tilts—we're going over! We cling in a big jumble of arms, hearts pounding in aching terror... then the vehicle straightens out... and we're driving along as though nothing happened.

"What the hell was that?" I choke.

"I don't know," Ruth sounds out of breath as well. "Maybe someone got out of one of the other trucks. I hope so."

"You think they jumped? On the *motorway?*"

"George Michael fell out of his car doing seventy on the motorway and had no serious injuries," Sasha tells us, voice quivering slightly with shock, her accent much thicker than normal.

"Lucky George Michael," I say sarcastically.

"Maybe the police are chasing us!" says Annabel.

"Why are we driving along innocently again, then?" I snap, 'cause I want it to be true, too, but I know it's not.

We sink back into silence. I can feel Ruth rearranging her hands and settling down to pray again. No way to tell how long it is before we slow, turn off. But it's not long. We drive a little further and then we stop.

They open the back door and herd us out. Two articulated lorries wait in a small unpaved parking area, looking huge and out of place. We're right in the middle of some woods, from the trees looming all around. I exchange looks with Ruth. The men seem so angry. Maybe someone did get away.

They make us stand in a group behind the horsebox and lower the ramp. There should be the better part of a hundred girls in there, unless my maths is wrong, but there's only, what, thirty or so? One of the men is in there already, standing in the doorway to the living area. The leader strides up the ramp. I think he's scowling, but it's hard to tell with that much beard in the way. He's ranting, there's no other word for it.

"So, *you let your friends escape!* You think you are worth the price of *two women each*, do you? Now *you* will do the work of two women! Who helped them? Did *you* help them? Did *you?*"

He begins rounding on trembling, crying girls, most of whom seem totally out of it with fear.

"Did you?" He grabs Frankie from year thirteen and she clearly seems slightly more with it because he smacks her across the face and shoves her into the grasp of the man next to him. "And you? Did you?"

15

"No! *No!*" But the fact Megan's capable of answering his question just seems to convince him she was in on the plan. Which is stupid. I mean, surely anyone who was in on the plan would've gone with the others?

"Tie them!" He shoves Megan to another man. "You lot, out!" he barks at the other girls. A couple of the men go in and drive them down the ramp like cattle, and when they're all out he turns to face us and yells, "Now you will find out what happens to disobedient women!" He points to Megan and Frankie, whose wrists have been tied to the horses' tethering rings, then waves towards the lorries.

"Put them all in one," he orders. "We'll dump the other in a lay-by somewhere."

Those who are quick enough manage to climb up into the truck by themselves; the slow ones are picked up and thrown in. No one gets a chance to run. I settle against a wall with Ruth and Annabel and Yoko. Annabel's trembling—Yoko's starting to look rather glazed, like she can't keep up with it all.

"What are they going to do to Megan and Frankie?" whispers Annabel.

I don't say anything. Two things come to mind and neither is good.

"Maybe they'll just... beat them," says Ruth, in the smallest voice I've ever heard from her. I never thought I'd hear her say the words 'just' and 'beat' in the same sentence, either, but I know exactly what she means.

But they don't 'just' beat them.

We hear the men go into the horsebox, one after the other.

We hear the screaming.

We can do nothing.

DANIYAH

When it's over, we sit in silence for what seems like forever. They don't bring Megan and Frankie back and we can't hear them anymore. Finally there's a few minutes of splashing outside, followed by a dim murmur.

16

They've purified themselves and they're praying. Dawn prayers.

I feel sick. I know I should do the same, but I can't even think of praying at the same time as them.

Eventually cab doors slam. Then we're moving again.

It feels like we drive for hours. The interior is dimly illuminated by daylight coming through a few tiny holes in the truck back, but we can't tell the time. After a couple of hours... half an hour?... who knows... my reason finally overcomes my emotions—I need to pray. Nothing changes that. But I have no water to perform *wudu*, or even any clean soil for a dry purification, and I don't know what to do.

Eventually I wrap my dressing gown around my head and bow down and pray anyway, though there's barely any room and I've no idea which way to face. A couple of girls boo and hiss—someone mutters, "Mrs Bin Laden!"

"Leave her alone," says a firm voice. Sounds like Ruth from the CU. She's only a year eleven, but people fall silent.

"She's no more deranged than she was yesterday," adds another voice. "And she's right here in this truck like the rest of us, isn't she?" It's that red-haired girl, Gemma, who can't talk to anyone without attacking their faith. It's odd to hear her standing up for me, though I know she's friends with Ruth.

When I've finished my prayers I notice the girl next to me is crying. A lot of girls are, but she's really crying, shoulders convulsing, though she's smothering the sound quite well. It's Becky, from the year above. The ballerina. I've seen her dance. I couldn't imagine wearing the outfit she had on—in public!—but she danced so beautifully...

"Are you... okay?" I whisper. Timidly. Maybe she won't want to talk to me.

"Yeah." But it's more of a whimper and her voice is choked with tears. After a moment's silence, she bursts out, "I *was* involved! I helped Ally plan it—the escape! I was just too scared to go myself. And I didn't say *anything*. I kept quiet and let them blame Megan and Frankie! And now... are they... *are they...?*"

"I don't know." My voice shakes and I try to find something comforting to say. "But if they're not... well, they're free, now. So they're the lucky ones, really."

"Lucky?" chokes Becky. "Didn't you *hear!*"

Just thinking about what I heard makes me want to vomit or faint. If that happens to me... how will I ever look my parents in the face again? "Yeah, but..." my voice shakes like a leaf, "We're probably going to get the same soon enough, only... without the benefit afterwards."

Becky's tears stop abruptly. "Are you trying to make me feel better?" She sounds strangled.

"Yeah," I say glumly.

She snorts, and then we're both laughing and sobbing and laughing and sobbing until my chest aches and we lean against each other, exhausted and just as scared as ever.

"I could've got away!" whispers Becky after a while. "I'm such a fool! Now I've missed my chance, like Ally said."

"They really jumped?"

"Yeah, about forty of them."

"Are they okay?"

"I don't know."

"Then... perhaps you shouldn't worry too much about not going with them. If you see what I mean..."

She gives a shaky laugh. "Yeah, I see what you mean... But I still wish I'd gone."

We sit in silence after that.

TERESA

Richford's marketplace clock strikes eight A.M. as I set up my music stand and choose something cheerful to start the day with.

Why does Dad always have to...? I push the thought away and pick up my violin—Mum's violin—and tune it carefully. All music should be the best one can make it. It's a form of prayer, really, the only one I indulge in as much as I should.

As usual, once I tuck my violin under my chin and begin to

play, the latest argument with my dad about going back to school and doing his precious science A levels falls away. I think of Mum instead, how she would listen to me play with her eyes half-closed, almost praying herself. I always feel like she's very close, when I play her violin.

I don't expect to earn much before lunchtime, but my violin case stays emptier than normal. Everyone's hurrying past, looking grim. When I stop to take out some more music and drink from my water bottle, I notice a crowd gathered in front of the TV shop and my stomach suddenly clenches into a knot.

It's too like that day when I was very little, when Mum took me into town to do some errands. We ended up stood outside a TV shop with a whole crowd of people staring at a telly in the window that was showing some boring adventure film— something about planes hitting a building.

It was only when one of the buildings collapsed—and I realized my Mum had her hand over her mouth and there were tears running down her face—that I realized it wasn't a film. It was *real*. And something in my world broke.

The crowd reminds me too much of that day. Has something happened? Another bomb? Not a big one, please... I pocket my meagre earnings, slip my violin into its case and put it over my shoulder, leaving my other things where they are, and jog along to the TV shop.

A picture of a burning building covers the screen, but it's some old country house, not a government building. My insides unknot slightly. It's just a big fire... then I see the headline scrolling across the screen:

BREAKING NEWS: 276 schoolgirls kidnapped from boarding school near Newbury

YOKO
I can't believe what's happening.
My parents told me for years that I would never get the

19

best job if I didn't speak English.

But I couldn't get the hang of it.

Then three months ago, they sat me down and told me they'd been saving for a long time and they thought they had enough to send me to the UK for one term at an English school, plus one month with a host family. A crash course. I was terrified—nothing like I'm feeling now—but I wanted to make them proud. Wanted to come back with basic English, at least. So I said I'd come.

But I've been here a month, and still I understand so little.

And now this...

I've figured it out.

These men aren't soldiers.

They're men like the ones they show on television here in England from time to time. On the news bulletins. The ones that make the girls talk in sad, serious voices and change the channel.

I know there's been a few bombs here. Even in Japan, we had one recently. But I didn't know they had these men in England. I thought they were somewhere over the sea. If *Chichi* and *Haha* had known, they'd never have made me come.

Except they didn't *make* me.

I press my hand against my dressing gown pocket and feel my *omamoris*, safe there. *Chichi* took me around all the best shrines to get them. He made sure I had one for safe travel and one for personal protection, but my favourite is the one for good education. I know the *kamis* will look after me as long as I have the *omamoris*.

But they're so far away, the *kamis*...

Oh, I wish I'd said no. I wish I'd said no. I wish I'd said no....

DANIYAH

After... who knows how long... someone touches my arm. "Daniyah?"

"*Louise?*" It's a mousy looking year ten I've never really talked to. "Why aren't you in Venice?"

She flushes slightly and mutters, "My parents couldn't afford it."

"That's... that's a real shame." Ten times the shame, now...

"Yeah," she says weakly. "Um, I thought maybe you should have this..." She pushes a pashmina into my hand. "I saw how they were with you back at school."

I stare at the scarf. A selfish part of me wants to take it, to seize anything that will make me a little safer... "You should keep it for yourself," I manage. "I don't wear a headscarf, anyway."

"If *you're* not going to wear it, *I'm* not!"

"Put it on!" calls Gemma from the other end of the truck. "Use your head, for pity's sake!"

I'm confused, but I bristle slightly. I've never liked Gemma and her incessant questions. I mean, does she think I'm an imam or something?

"Gemma's right. You should put it on," comes Ruth's gentler voice. "If you get into their good graces—assuming they have any—you may be able to help the rest of us, even if it's just by escaping and telling someone where we are. I'm guessing the police haven't a clue about that, by now."

Gemma says *shhh* rather loudly, clearly afraid this is too much truth for some people to hear.

They're right, though, so I wrap the scarf around my head as best I can and tuck it in to try and make it stay.

"Next time we stop," says Becky from beside me, "why don't you bang on the door and get them to let you out to pray with them? You might get a chance to make a break for it."

I sigh. "Women pray in private, Becky, not with men— according to people like them, anyway. So I'm afraid that's a really bad idea."

"They'd shoot her just for suggesting it," snorts Gemma.

Unfortunately, for once Gemma is right.

RISHAD

I wake up with this nagging unease chewing at my belly. I

sit up and frown. I was dreaming... but it was a nice dream. I scramble out of bed and hurry to Isaar's room, but his bed's neatly made. He sits down to pray and read the Quran after we return from dawn prayer, no matter how late we study in the evening, my preferred use of the time too, but there's a limit to how much sleep I can miss and still be safe in a lab. But he's gone downstairs now, as usual.

"Isaar?" I call, taking the stairs two at a time. "Isaar, what's wrong?"

No answer. I hurry to the living room. Isaar's kneeling in front of the TV as though he became so enrapt by what he was watching the thought of moving to a chair didn't even enter his mind.

"What is it?" I demand, because all I can see on screen is some big fire at a country mansion, and why that would be upsetting him this much...

He's not hearing me. I cross the room and scoop up his phone, abandoned beside him. Press my finger to the scanner— the only thing we can't fool, other than our mum. It's set to unlock for me, though, and as I expected, I'm looking at a news page. I swipe to the top and read the headline. Read it again.

BREAKING NEWS: 280 SCHOOLGIRLS KIDNAPPED FROM UK SCHOOL

My hands begin to shake. I drop down beside Isaar on the carpet and start staring at the screen as well. I don't need to ask him who's responsible. I knew *who* as soon as I saw him kneeling here, radiating anguish. The same people who've been rampaging around the world since we were boys, bent on blackening our faith beyond all redemption. Or so it sometimes feels.

Other times, usually in the middle of the night when I hope no angels are watching my thoughts, I find myself wondering if here in the UK we haven't Christianized our faith to accommodate it to our British values. But I would never admit that to anyone, not even Isaar. Because the cold, harsh version of our faith that seems to be held in other parts of the world— that *can't* be true Islam—that's not a faith I could ever die for— and it's definitely not a faith I can live for. Or believe in. Or anything.

I think of Allah, all merciful, all compassionate, and as always the doubt flies back into the night where it belongs. I concentrate on the news—a presenter stands in front of the burning school, firemen rushing around in the background.

"Chisbrook Hall is a Methodist boarding school, originally intended for the daughters of Methodist ministers, who move church every five years. Most of the pupils nowadays come from families of all faiths and none, but the school has a vibrant Christian Union, headed by Alleluia Williams, the daughter of an American pastor currently working in the Middle East. Alleluia—known as Ally to her friends—has now been confirmed to be among the forty-nine girls who jumped out of a horsebox on the M4 a couple of hours ago. All forty-nine have been taken to hospital and their parents have been informed.

"The two hundred and twenty-seven girls who remain missing are mostly aged sixteen to eighteen years old, with the exception of two girls from year ten, aged just fourteen and fifteen. In what school staff and parents are already describing as a 'miracle', the four youngest year groups were all away on school trips. Day pupils from year eleven have already been informed by the exam board that they will not have to sit their Physics GCSE this morning.

"We're joined by Mrs Ruttridge, whose daughter, Alice, is in year eleven, but was not at school last night. Mrs Ruttridge, how did you feel when you heard the news?"

A white-faced lady appears on screen, her arm locked around what must be her daughter—the girl's face is blurred out. "Just... shock. Total and utter shock. I'm still finding it hard to believe it. A fire, yes, but... I know there've been a lot of bombs recently, but... *this*..."

"And does Alice ever stay over at school?"

"Yes, frequently. She wanted to stay last night, ready for the exam, but her father and I decided in the end..." the woman's voice is shaking wildly, "we decided she should stay at home and get a good night's sleep... I'm not religious, but all I can think is *thank you, thank you, thank you!*" She looks around at the sky in a rather confused manner, but I feel no inclination to laugh.

"Thank you, Mrs Ruttridge," says the presenter, and the woman is allowed to move away with her daughter. He begins to go through what's clearly a preliminary list of some of the kidnapped girls—there are some foreign pupils, several girls whose parents are out of the country on mission—but they've all now been contacted—one Muslim girl—*why was she taken?* they ask—might as well ask why any of them were taken! There's a Jewish girl at the school as well, but she was in Venice on one of the trips, so that's something—they're all flying home straight away, etc.

I look at Isaar. He's taking it all in, every detail cutting him like a knife. "I don't think there's much point watching all this. They don't know anything more, yet."

He doesn't really hear me. I get up and go to the door, yell up the stairs, "Sam? Have you seen this?" No answer. I check my watch. Eight forty-five. Sam has a nine o'clock tutorial. He's already gone out.

Isaar looks round at last, though, his eyes too big, like he's in shock. Probably is. I feel a bit like someone sloshed a bucket of cold water over me.

"Come on, Isaar. Don't torture yourself. There's nothing we can do."

His face screws up in pain. "That makes it easier for you, does it? For me it makes it worse..." He doesn't move from the floor, so I reach for the off button on the TV remote...

"...All army units are being mobilized to search for the vehicles used in the kidnapping, which investigators believe will now have been abandoned. Examination of the site may provide valuable information about the vehicles into which the girls have been transferred, and their destination. All soldiers currently on leave are requested, though not required, to report back to their unit to take part. Civilians are not being invited to take part in the search at this time..."

Isaar puts his hand in his pocket, looking for his phone. I'm still holding it. In fact, I've already swiped through to 'contacts' and found the right number.

It's picked up on the third ring. "Sergeant-Major Wood, Oxford University Officer Training Corps, who is it?"

"Officer Cadet Iqbal. Is the OTC helping with the search?"

"Hang on, I'm busy, but Major Lewington's here, I'll pass you over." His voice gets fainter. "Sir? Officer Cadet Iqbal."

"Which one?"

"Er... Isaar." Just checked what his phone's telling him.

"Iqbal?" The CO's voice.

"Yes, sir. Well, no, it's Rishad, actually. Shall we come in to help search?"

"Yes. The sergeant-major is preparing a text message and email as we speak. Transport will be leaving HQ in one hour. Anyone able to take part is to be in uniform so the public know it's official."

"Isaar and I are in, then. Officer Cadet Worthing, too." There wasn't a tutorial on the planet Sam wouldn't walk out of for something like this.

"Good. But, Officer Cadet Iqbal?"

"Yes, sir?"

"You and... Officer Cadet Iqbal... will have to stay with the minibus and man the radio."

"What! Why?"

"That's the orders from the MOD. Any soldier who looks as though they might be Muslim is to take a support role in this operation."

"*But...!*"

"It's been all over the news that the terrorists were masquerading as soldiers. Do you really want your twin pumped full of lead shot by an angry farmer who jumps to the wrong conclusion?"

I press my lips together as that familiar anger boils inside.

Once again, the acts of evil men rebound on us. Why doesn't Allah strike all the heretics down dead and be done with it? I push that thought aside too, and say, "Of course not, sir. We'll be there within an hour."

"Good man. Bring any of the others you can."

"Yes, sir."

He hangs up. For a moment I stare at my reflection in the shiny screen of the phone. At the brown skin and neat little beard that relegates us to minding the radio. I find myself thinking of that day when we woke up as British boys who happened to be Muslim and went to bed Muslim boys who happened to be British—not that we realized right away.

"We can help, right? So what's wrong?" Isaar looks with-it again, raring to go now there's something he can do.

"We have to stay with the transport and babysit the radio."

"Why?" he says blankly.

"Trigger-happy farmers." I trace my fingers around my beard and he gets it. From his frown, he's every bit as unhappy as I am, but being Isaar, he just remains silent for rather too long and then says, "Well, I suppose…"

I know what's coming and say it with him. "…Someone *does* need to mind the radio."

ANNABEL

How long have we been driving? Gemma's bored. I can tell because she's just interrupted Ruth's prayers and they're at it again. I don't know how Ruth stays friends with Gemma sometimes. The Holy Spirit, I suppose.

Sasha's telling me about the latest trials and tribulations of her favourite boy band whilst determinedly trying to get the knots out of her frizz, a tall order without her brush. What she's saying would be slightly interesting in other circumstances but it seems utterly meaningless now.

I feel trapped between two equally tedious conversations. I plait my hair. Un-plait it. Plait it again…

"How could he possibly be watching over us right now?"

Gemma is demanding. "How could he let this happen?"

"He respects free will, Gemma," says Ruth patiently. From the way she keeps thumb pressed to one finger, she was saying a rosary and is trying to remember her place. I've never got into the whole rosary thing. Not very Anglican. "Those horrible men have free will, same as us. That's why he has to let bad things happen. But he always brings good out of everything."

"*Good?* Where's the good in *this?*"

"Well, I'd call the absence of four year groups of younger girls a great good, myself."

"That was coincidence."

"One of God's favourite tools. Not a very subtle coincidence, in this case. I mean, when did year ten leave?"

"This morning. I mean, yesterday morning."

"And when are year seven coming back?"

"Tomorr... this afternoon."

"Exactly. So for one single night, there were fewer girls in the school than there have ever been on any night in the entire time we've been at Chisbrook. The most away at the same time previously has been what, two year groups together? And this is the night those evil men carry out their evil plan?"

"I thought you didn't like calling people evil."

"You're right, I should probably say they're utterly deluded or something. I'm just having trouble believing it so I feel like I'd be lying."

"You would be lying," snorts Gemma.

"I think your pants would be on fire," I can't help saying.

Sasha sniffs indignantly, realizing I'm not listening to her.

"How can anyone pray five times a day or however many it is and not figure out that God doesn't want them to rape and murder...?" I break off, scared of the words that have just come from my mouth. They seem far too real, filling the back of the truck like looming black shadows.

"Hey, I think we're turning off..." says Sasha, forgetting to be huffy.

27

GEMMA

I kind of don't want them to open those doors... but at the same time, I do. There's a limit to how long one wants to sit in the back of a truck, in semi-darkness, with nothing to do but feel mad at Ruth. And there's no way out of here, no hope at all of 'doing an Ally', as people are calling it.

How I feel about it doesn't matter, of course. They open the doors.

The truck's stopped on a narrow track in an area of long grass waving in the wind. Actually... I scuff one sore foot on the ground. Sand dunes. When I sniff, I smell the sea.

"If anyone runs," the leader is shouting, "we will shoot you. No one will pay any attention—many wild fowl live here and people are out shooting them every day. Walk and keep your mouths shut."

We set off along a path leading into the dunes. The truck starts up and drives away—they're going to dump it somewhere else. Surely someone will see us? One glimpse, and they'll report it, surely? Over two hundred girls in nightwear, men with guns? Surely someone will see?

But the area is deserted. Sea birds wheel and call to one another—nothing human stirs as far as the eye can see. Soon we're descending a sort of gully, and there is the sea, ahead. Oh no, they're going to put us on a ship, aren't they? Everyone will be searching the UK from top to bottom, and we'll be half way to who knows where...

The gully comes out into a small, pebbly inlet. We wobble and totter over the rocks towards the sea. A large speedboat is waiting and when we reach the water's edge the men force us onwards. The water is icy cold and soaks straight through our nightclothes. The girls at the front are up to their waists already. Yoko gives a frightened meep and stops to take something from her pocket, carries on with her cupped hands held high in the air.

What on earth has she got... Oh no! I bet she grabbed her charms from her little bedside shrine—you don't leave sacred objects made of paper and wood in a burning building...

I try to wade faster, to catch her up, to make her put them out of sight again even if they get wet, but the water is too deep, the waves too strong and there are too many girls in the way.

"Ruth..." I hiss. We're getting close to the boat and don't want the men to hear me. "*Ruth!*"

She looks round at last.

"Yoko's got her... *things...*" I don't dare shout about amulets and talismans. "She needs to put them away!"

Ruth looks puzzled—looks round and sees Yoko with her arms in the air. Understanding covers her face—and fear. She lurches through the water and tries to pull Yoko's arms down, whispering to her urgently. Yoko shakes her head and pulls free—doesn't understand or isn't prepared to get them wet, or both. I redouble my efforts to catch up, but fortunately Ruth is edging Yoko along the boat so they won't have to climb in right by one of the men.

Ruth gets up into the boat first and tries to haul Yoko up, but it's not working—Yoko is only prepared to take one hand from the charms. One of the men begins to head towards her to pull her in—I get there in time to put a shoulder under her and shove her up into the boat. The man turns back to someone else.

Phew. I think we may be okay.

RUTH

"Yoko, please put them away," I whisper. The wind is whipping my brown hair across my face. I claw it back and point to Yoko's pocket to help her understand. "Put them away, now, *please!*"

Yoko shakes her head, confused and a bit annoyed. "Wet," she says, squishing a bit of the wet fabric in her free hand. "Wet, look! No good."

"The men mustn't see them, Yoko," Gemma whispers, her short red hair blowing upright like a mane. "They must not see them! Put them away! They won't get as wet as they would have done in the sea!"

29

Yoko doesn't understand this; she just shakes her head again. "Keep safe!" She wipes her hand on the top of her shoulder—the only dry place—and wraps it back around the talismans. "From my *Kamis*. I keep safe."

"The men will take them away." I almost add that they will probably do something awful to Yoko as well, but it'll be too many words. She won't understand. "They will take them. You have to put them away to keep them safe. Put away—keep safe, understand? We can dry them later."

"Wet!" says Yoko. She looks like she's about to cry. She doesn't understand and me having a go at her, as she sees it, is clearly the last straw.

I put an arm around her quickly. "Shss, don't cry. Just hold them, then. Down here," I gently press her hands into her lap. "Don't wave them around, okay?"

She sniffs into my shoulder a bit, promptly clutching the charms to her chest again.

Gemma shifts to try and hide her from the men as much as possible. "Sit there, Annabel," she says, as Annabel sloshes over the side of the boat and starts trying to wring out her hair.

"Why?"

"Yoko brought her charms," I whisper. "She won't put them back in her pocket because they'll get wet."

"So?"

"So, we mustn't let the men see them."

"Why not?"

"Were you awake in R.E. the other week?" says Gemma under her breath. "When we learnt about Shinto in honour of Yoko's arrival? Those charms are something to do with some kind of spirit nature deities—it's serious polytheism, Shinto."

Annabel looks a bit blank, so I whisper, "Worshipping multiple gods."

Annabel bites her lip and her eyes slide sideways to look at the nearest terrorist. "They don't like that, do they?"

"No, so we've got to keep those charms hidden."

"She should chuck them overboard," says Gemma.

"Probably not a bad idea," says Annabel.

30

"I'd agree, only... I don't know how important those things are," I say. "Would you be prepared to... chuck the Blessed Sacrament overboard, for example?"

"I'd eat it."

"Yeah, I know, but you see my point. She's not going to do it, anyway, and if we try and take them, she'll make a scene. Anyway, how are we better than them, if we take them by force?"

"You over-think things, Ruth," says Gemma. "She needs to get rid of them."

"Perhaps she can hide them when we get on the ship."

There's a black silhouette further out to sea, a much larger vessel. Most likely it's where we're headed.

"Where do you think they're taking us?" asks Annabel.

Somewhere wild and isolated, where people are prepared to buy and sell girls. I keep my mouth shut.

Everyone's on board now—the boat is packed. The man who was bringing up the rear climbs in—they'll start the engines now and we'll be gone. I eye the beach and think about going overboard. But Yoko won't come, and Annabel and most of the others probably won't catch on quick enough, and anyway, there really doesn't seem to be anyone around, so they probably would just shoot us.

The man walks up the boat, kicking anyone who gets in his way, and stops in front of us. In front of Yoko

"Show me," he snaps.

YOKO

I try to understand the man's words. He wants to see something. Was this what Ruth was trying to tell me? That the men want to see my *omamoris*?

The man grabs my hands, wrenches them apart, and my *omamoris* scatter over the wet decking. A cry escapes me and I kneel to gather them up, but the man's hand slams across my face, knocking me back against Ruth. He bends to grab the nearest one, shakes it in my face, yelling.

31

What is he saying... he wants to know what it is...

"From *Kami*," I tell him, trying to reach the ones still on the floor. "From home mountain Kami. This..." I manage to grab my *gakugyō-jōju*, my most precious *omamori*, "bring good education..." I've almost got the next one when he stamps on my hand.

I scream in pain and recoil again, cradling my throbbing hand and the *gakugyō-jōju* to my chest. The man is shouting something that sounds like, "shirk," which is what the girls say if someone isn't doing their share of the dorm chores. He's practically foaming at the mouth. I shrink against Ruth, terrified. I didn't mean to be a shirker... When did they tell me to do chores?

He holds the *omamori* in front of me, pulls out his knife and stabs the little cloth pouch, rips it open. I see the paper of the amulet inside and know the protection is gone.

"*Iie! Iie! No!*" the cry bursts out. He's grabbing the others from the floor now, ripping them open... I try to reach them, but Ruth has got her arms around me, holding me. "Stop, Yoko, stop," she's whispering... that's it, that's the word I'm looking for...

"Stop!" I shout. "Stop! No do this! Bad! Stop!"

He's shouting even louder than me. He wants me to say something, but the words he says are totally incomprehensible.

"Say it!" Gemma's yelling. "Just say it, Yoko!"

Say what? He's not making any sense, keeps saying something in a language I've never even heard. He reaches for my *gakugyō-jōju*—it's for good education, not personal protection, but it's the only one I have left—I clutch it tight. He grabs it and yanks. I hold on.

"Let it go!" Gemma's screaming it, so's Annabel. And something about what it's worth, or not worth... I can't understand; I'm too busy hanging onto my *omamori*. The man is shouting something I don't understand and waving the knife. Ruth's screaming now, right in my ear though she's talking to the man...

"She doesn't understand! Please, *listen to me!* She's not

saying no! She doesn't *understand what you're saying*! *LISTEN...*"

The man lashes out with the knife. I feel an impact across my throat and a terrible, sharp pain... then I'm choking, something hot is pouring into my windpipe and I'm choking, drowning, my hands flail but darkness is spiralling in around me and somehow I've slumped right onto the decking and Ruth's shouting "it's going to be okay, Yoko, it's going to be okay," and it makes me feel a little better but I'm choking, choking and there's a tide of bright blood flowing over my ruined *omamoris* and if that's all coming from me I really hope someone's called... called an...

GEMMA

Yoko's lying there on the deck with her eyes wide open and blank, totally blank, there's blood everywhere and I can only stare at her... I was afraid this would probably happen to someone... but... but...

Ruth's screaming at the man, screaming at him, I've never seen her so angry, she's shaking her fist, tears tracking through the blood that's sprayed over her face. Annabel grabs her and tries to pull her back into her seat, to calm her, and I finally snap out of my paralysis and reach for her as well... too slow, the man smacks her across the face with the back of his hand and only my lunge stops her going overboard.

She slumps down on the bench—stunned into silence, thank goodness—stares at her hands, red with blood... Begins to sob.

"Quiet!" shouts the man, and the noise in the boat drops a little. "Allah does not tolerate idolatry! Anyone who refuses to repent of *shirk* will die, just like this infidel bitch." He kicks Yoko's body and for a horrible moment I think Ruth's about to throw herself at him.

For a moment I think I am too.

ANNABEL

I can't believe this. He just killed Yoko over a handful of oversized phone charms, or that's what they always looked like to me. If only there was something we could've done to make her understand...

Ruth's gone back to crying. I'm not sure if I've ever seen her cry before. Not like this. I just feel numb. But Miss Trott asked Ruth to look after Yoko when she arrived. Ruth's good at things like that. Miss Trott never expected her to fight off madmen with knives, but I doubt Ruth sees it like that.

I want to try and comfort her, but she's covered in Yoko's blood and I really don't want any more on me. But... Gemma's still staring at the terrorist like a hungry lioness so, gingerly, I slip an arm around Ruth.

The terrorist goes over to the leader and a couple of the others—they slap him on the back approvingly, murmur *"Allahu akbar!"* Then they start the engines and we're off, skimming over the waves towards that gloomy silhouette.

SASHA

The wind knifes through my wet dressing down and I sit and shake as we roar along. To start with I try to hold onto my hair, frizzy enough at the best of times, but it's no use. This is going to be the bad hair day of all bad hair days. I'm going to look like that female drummer from... what's the band called? Yet again my eyes wander right back to the still form sprawled in a sea of brilliant red, near the front of the boat. My stomach churns and churns, until eventually I have to hang over the side of the boat and vomit.

I can't bear looking anymore. At anything. I press my face to my knees, wrap my arms around my head and stay like that until a gentle bump reverberates through the boat and men start calling from above in a foreign language. Arabic?

Raising my head from my knees to look at the ship, the first thing I see is a rivulet of pink-tinged water, lapping around my shoe. My stomach heaves and I throw up right there by my feet. I look around quickly, fear catching my breath. Did the men see? Will they be angry?

They're not paying any attention to me. One of them made a much bigger mess in the boat, anyway. With a huge effort, I manage not to look at Yoko again and stumble to my feet as the nearest man starts yelling, "Up! Up!"

We're moored beside a proper ship. It's a fraction of the size of a container ship, maybe the size of a ferry? I don't know much about ships, but it still seems huge. The men make us climb rope ladders to reach the deck—I'm so cold and stiff I'm afraid I'll fall, but I make it. I'm still shaking as I climb over the side.

A man I haven't seen before jerks me to my feet, shoves an armful of fabric into my arms and pushes me after the girl in front. I follow blindly, stumbling into the girl—Louise from year ten—when she finally stops. We're in the hold, by the look of it. There are jerry cans of water and washing up bowls on the floor.

"Get in here!" A man pushes Daniyah past me, looking weird with a purple pashmina wrapped around her head, then turns to face the rest of us. "Listen up, all of you. We chose you because you are Christians. We know you have been badly brought up and you believe in three Gods. If you carry on with this belief, you will stay in hell forever. But now you are here with us you have the chance to accept Islam and live good lives and make honourable marriages. You have been given decent clothing. Put it on. A good *Muslimah* shows only her face and hands. Anyone who shows their hair, or their neck, or their wrists, or their feet or ankles, is a whore and will be treated as such."

He swings back to Daniyah. "Replace that gaudy thing and help the others. Anyone who's not decent in half an hour will get what they deserve."

Daniyah stands and trembles for a moment, then finds her voice. "They can't... they can't wash with... with men here..."

"Just get on with it; your half hour's started."

Daniyah edges away from the man—for a moment she just

stands and trembles. "Um... everyone?" she calls. Her voice shakes too. I can't tell if she's more scared of the men or of having to tell us what to do. "We've been given clothes. We need to wash—just... just do anywhere that's dirty—then put the clothes on. The robe thing goes first, then you put this around your head," she holds up a short scarfy thing, "and then pull the thing with a hole in on over the top. If anyone's not sure, I can help. All your hair needs to be under the scarf, okay?"

"I thought you didn't wear *hijab?*" snaps Jenny from year thirteen.

"My granny does," says Daniyah weakly.

"If you've got a better idea how to do it, step up," says Becky sarcastically, pirouetting gracefully towards the bowls.

People begin to follow her. *Anywhere that's dirty...* I think that's code for *I know you're all wet, but don't take your kit off.* Like we would, with all those men watching our every move. When I get a turn at the bowl I wash my face quickly and move away again.

The robe is like a bin liner, it's the most unflattering thing I've ever seen, let alone put on. I can't believe I actually have to wear it. It goes all the way to the floor and more, I don't know how I'll walk around, let alone do anything. I *so* need a pair of high heels. I wrap the scarf around my head and tie it at the back of my neck, then pull the hood-thing over my head. The bottom of the hole goes under my chin and the top rests on the scarf. Acres of fabric seem to cascade over my arms, I feel smothered, stifled... My hair is invisible. Almost all of me is invisible. I feel... erased.

"Good, Sasha, good," Daniyah appears in front of me, peering nervously at my headgear. "You'll be fine..." She hurries on to the next girl.

My hands paw at the fabric, trying to find their way out. I clutch my head, slip my fingers into the neck of the hood-thing, try to loosen it. It feels like a noose. How long will I have to wear this for?

I work a finger in under the scarf and hook out a lock of

hair. Do the same on the other side. The ringlets tickle my face and I can breathe again. I stare at my pink fingernails. They haven't got chipped yet.

I'm still here. Still Sasha.

GEMMA

Annabel and I wash as quickly as we can, because Ruth's sat on the floor with her head on her knees and she's clearly going to need help.

"Leave it," I mutter to Annabel—she's still scrubbing at the bloodstains on her dressing gown.

"I need to get it off..." Her voice has a frantic edge to it.

I catch her arm. "*Leave it*. It's not going to come out."

"I'll take it off, then, I've got the robe..."

"Do you see any heaters in here?" We're all shivering violently in our wet things. "We should keep on every stitch we've got; the robes are thin as. Just put the thing on over the top and try to forget it. But let's leave those head getups until we've got Ruth sorted out."

We scramble into the sacks—sorry, robes—and I immediately wish we'd left those off for now as well, even if they do make us a tiny bit warmer. But the half hour is ticking away, so we hitch them up and get back to Ruth, taking one of the bowls of water with us.

Despite what I just said about heating, I don't see how Ruth can keep her dressing gown on—it's soaked in blood. As long as we can hold onto it, maybe we can wash it, or brush the worst off once it's dry.

"Ruth? Ruth, come on, you need to wash..." She's shivering particularly hard, whether from cold or shock, who knows. I untie her dressing gown cord and peel the gory thing off her, but the blood's soaked right through and her nightdress is red with it.

"What do we do?" asks Annabel. She's gone very white and keeps looking away from the blood and then back again. "Should we take it off?"

"You've got to be joking." I roll my eyes in the direction of the watching men. "*No way, Jose.* Though... actually... see if you can get that pashmina from Daniyah, would you?"

Annabel wades away in her sack and I start cleaning the blood from Ruth's face. After a few swipes of the sponge she puts her hand up and takes it from me, starts washing herself. She does her hands and arms and neck, and wipes her hair off as well as she can, then drops the sponge back in the pink water, stares down at her nightie and says in a tiny voice, "Oh..." She uses a word I've never heard her use before.

"We'll sort it out," I say quickly, because a few more tears are trickling down her cheeks.

Annabel comes back with the purple thing, so I hunt around until I find a jagged rivet in the floor I can hook the centre of the scarf around, to tear a hole in it. I knot the corners together and have an extremely makeshift... shift.

"Let's go in that corner and you can get this on," I tell Ruth.

She gets up slowly, as though she can hardly remember how, but follows us. Annabel and I hold out our voluminous robes to make a screen while she peels off the gory garment, has a quick splash with the water and pulls on the skimpy pashmina robe.

"Quick!" I kick the pile of grey-black garments towards her with my foot. "There's a man coming, get them on..."

"What you do?" demands the man. One of the new ones. The foreign ones.

"She's washing and dressing, as ordered." Somehow I manage to keep my voice respectful.

"Let me see..." he shoves me out the way—but Ruth has the robe on and is trying to figure out what to do with her grey scarf. "Get back with others!" he snaps, dragging us roughly across the big metal room. Disappointed he didn't get an eyeful, the perv.

"Get your headscarves on!" says Daniyah, hurrying up to us as he sulks back off to join the other men. "It must be nearly half an hour."

I tie the scarf around my head and tuck my hair in carefully. I'm not giving those bastards any excuse to hurt me. The hood is horrible, tight under my chin and enveloping around my arms. Ruth stares at hers for a long moment before pulling it on. Maybe it's shock and grief slowing her thought processes, but I've a nasty feeling it's just her deciding where she draws the line and whether this is or isn't it.

Apparently it isn't. I'd thank God for that, if I thought he existed.

SASHA

"So," shouts the leader, "Now we will see which of you may make good *Muslimah* and which are fit only to be slaves! Line up, all of you."

We stumble into rows, tripping over our dragging hems. Everyone looks like sinister grey ghosts in the ugly get-up. The man walks up and down slowly, staring at everyone's face, glancing up and down their bodies.

"Good..." he murmurs now and then. "Excellent..." The new men look disappointed every time he says it.

My stomach gurgles and suddenly I'm aware of how hungry I am. We've eaten nothing all day. Surely after this inspection they'll give us some food?

The man is approaching. My ringlets are tickling my face... it's just two little locks, but... no one else has ringlets. Maybe I *should* tuck them in. Just until this is over... I reach up and try to shove them under the scarf, but I've tied it too tight and my fingers are too cold. There... they're basically in. I lower my hands and stand still as the man appears in front of me.

"Well, what do we have here?" He grabs a tuft of hair and yanks it out by the roots—I cry out in pain, my hand flying to the spot. "A whore! Showing her hair! Oh yes," he grabs my hand and holds it aloft, displaying my nails, "a proper painted western whore! Here, this one is a slave..."

He grabs a handful of my robe and propels me towards the group of men from the ship. When he lets me go I try to get back to everyone else, but the men start shoving me from one to the other, start putting their hands on me...

"Stop it! Please stop it!" I gasp. "I'll tuck my hair in, I promise! I didn't mean any harm! Please, leave me alone..."

"She want to show hair!" sneers one. "Whore!" He grabs my hood-thing and drags it off. Suddenly I want it back, want it desperately. I make a grab for it, but he throws it aside. Another man rips the scarf off my head, taking more hair with it. I grab for that, too, but it's no use.

"Whore!" "Whore!" the men hiss. One of them pulls me back against him and puts his hands... everywhere. A scream wrenches from me and I begin to struggle...

Dimly I hear the leader yelling. "Stand still and shut up, all of you! The next one to speak out of turn joins the slave girl, understand? The rest of you look like you might make good *Muslimah*. From now on keep your mouths shut and do as you're told, and you will make honourable marriages..."

The men are dragging me out of the hold, touching me, touching me all over, and I'm screaming, "Help me! Help me!" but there's no one who can help me, no one...

The hold door slams behind us and now there's no one who can hear me either...

No one who cares.

SAM

We've spent hours trailing through any bit of woodland that can be accessed by road and we're scratched and footsore and frustrated. And hot. The sun was beating down before we even got off the minibus. Of course we know ninety-nine point nine percent of the searchers in the entire country won't find anything *and* we're being given the least likely areas, what with us being, like, Britain's eighty-eighth line of defence or something—but I suppose we're all hoping—and dreading what we might find, at the same time.

At such short notice, on a weekday in June, the University Officer Cadets could only muster two platoons. Not bad really, seeing that most of the third years were too busy with Finals to come and the first years have exams too. Major Lewington stuck me in charge of the second platoon at once—since I'm off to Sandhurst in couple of weeks to do my officer training.

Thinking about that makes me excited and nervous at the same time. I'll be a proper officer by next term, assuming I don't flunk out. I'm on an army bursary, so when I got Rish's text I excused myself from my tutorial right away. Actually, I'd have excused myself right away anyway...

Movement up ahead... my mind snaps back to the job at hand, heart lurching in hope-fear. It'll be nothing... it'd better be nothing, we're all unarmed... Take more than this for them to issue live ammo to university students.

The biggest excitement of the morning approaches... in the form of a teenage boy riding bareback—and barefooted—on a black and white pony. He rides right on up to our fatigue-clad selves in a way that makes me pretty sure he's heard nothing about the terrorists. A couple of dead rabbits hang down one side of the pony's neck and as he comes closer I see two pheasants and a hare hanging on the other side. I look a bit askance at those—game, not vermin.

He sees my look. "I'm on my way to the farmhouse," he tells me straightforwardly, but with a touch of impatience and a roll of his eyes. "Mr Matthews will choose what he wants and I'll have the rest. I'm not poaching."

"Did I say anything?"

"You were thinking it."

I have to smile at his plain-speaking. From the scratching sounds coming from the box-like bag he's wearing, there's something alive in there... But what it is isn't relevant to the mission. All the same, I can't help asking, "Why aren't you in school?"

"I don't go to school. I'm home-schooled. Or..." He grins. "Caravan-schooled."

"Oh, you're a gyp... traveller, right?"

"Half. My dad's a hippie. Traveller-wannabee, as my mum would say."

"Right. Well... Have you seen any horseboxes or vans back there in the woods?"

He gives me a funny look. "You're soldiers, right? Why are you looking for vans?"

"Yes, territorial army, strictly speaking—but we're just university officer cadets. We're looking for the two hundred and seventy-six schoolgirls who were kidnapped this morning. Or rather, the vehicles they were taken in, almost certainly abandoned, by now."

The boy greets this with a nod. "So this is like a role-play, or something, right? That you're doing for training? Is it okay for me to tell you where they are, then, or are you supposed to find them yourselves?"

"No, they've really been taken. By Islamist fanatics... Wait, are you saying you've *seen* some vans back there?"

"Yeah," he says slowly, eyes very wide. Then he shakes his head as though to banish his shock and turns the pony, puts it to a canter, calling over his shoulder, "This way..."

"Wait!" I yell. "You need to wait for us. Those men are dangerous."

He pulls the pony to a halt and looks us up and down. "And what are you going to do, spit at them?"

I try not to grit my teeth too hard. "We can at least make a cautious approach," I tell him, then call to the others, "Okay, stay in your line but we're following the pony. Double-time."

As we jog through the woods, sweat trickling down our necks, I try to radio Rish and Isaar, to give an update on our movements. But all I get is static. Something wrong with the radio. The OTC gets issued with all the rubbish. Understandable, but it doesn't stop it being irritating sometimes. I pull out my phone instead, but there's no signal. With a sigh, I put it away again. It's not like we're leaving our search area, by the look of it, and it's almost certainly nothing.

When the boy slips from the pony's back and throws his reins over a bush, we catch him up. "This way," he whispers, and glides off silently through the trees.

We follow, sounding like a herd of blundering elephants in

comparison. But we soon come over a slight rise and there below us is a clearing...

My heart begins to pound. Three vehicles. Two white vans and a blue horsebox... God help us, it's an exact match! I hesitate, torn. We're under strict orders to call for armed backup if we find anything, but... I try the radio again. Nothing. No signal on my phone still. What have we got to report, anyway? There doesn't seem to be anyone here. It may be nothing to do with the kidnapping.

"Wrexham, come with me," I say softly. "We'll circle the clearing and see what we can see. Everyone else, stay here. Tanner, you're in charge. If someone shoots us, bug out and phone for help as soon as you can get a signal."

I pick up a sturdy branch and move down the slope towards the clearing. A stick's better than nothing, right? Henry Wrexham follows. The gypsy-boy has slipped all the way to the edge of the clearing and is peering from behind a bush. I'd better try and get him to stay back.

But as I move down towards him, I find that I can see the backs of the vehicles, and they're all open, the roll backs up on the vans and the ramp down on the horsebox. A prickle of unease runs up my spine. Okay, so it's really hot today, but it could just as easily be chucking it down with rain. Why would someone leave their vehicles open like that? Especially since the locked gate between the clearing and the track makes it unlikely they've just been parked up there for an hour or two.

The boy glances at me when I stop beside him. "Someone brought a really big vehicle up into this clearing sometime this morning," he tells me softly, pointing. "You can see the tyre marks. Looks like an articulated lorry. Totally unsuitable for that track."

Another cold prickle. Okay, according to our orders, we should now report it, even if we have to go all the way back to the minibus to do it...

"Change of plan, Henry," I say. "We'll..."

"Help..." The thin cry comes from the horsebox, and the despairing note to it suggests the person has been calling now

and then for a long time and no longer has any hope of getting a response.

"There's someone in there!" cries the boy, and he's off like a whippet across the clearing and up the ramp of the horsebox.

Swallowing a curse, I rush after him, but he's standing at the top of the ramp, staring in horror. I look past him, and my heart seems to stop. In the dimness of the horsebox's interior, I can make out two girls, slumped with their legs out in front of them, their wrists tied to rings on the walls, holding them upright. Bare scraps of clothing cover their bruised bodies, and blood coats their...

I step backwards, wanting to get away from the scene, and almost lose my footing on the ramp. The stumble brings me to my senses. Henry's rushing up the ramp as well, and I force myself to look inside the horsebox again. Relief swamps me as I see their chests rise and fall. They're alive.

"Has anyone got a knife?" My voice sounds strange.

Henry stops dead, gasping, but the boy pulls a hunting knife from his belt and offers it to me.

"Right," I say, taking it. I move forward, but as my shadow falls over one of the girls she lifts her head, sees me and flinches back, a feeble sound of terror coming from her throat. Since I've a pretty good idea what the last fatigue-clad man she saw did to her, I back out, turn around and look to the tree line instead. "Tanner, Philpott," I call. "And... I can't remember your name, sorry. Down here, please. But don't walk over those tyre tracks."

The three Woman Officer Cadets come jogging over—the others following them.

"No," I shout, "everyone else, *stay there*. You'll walk on the evidence." I offer the knife to Hattie Tanner, who is now staring into the horsebox, white-faced. "I want you three to cut them loose and look after them," I tell her, slipping out of my combat smock and handing it to Phillie. "Here, one of them can have that."

Henry quickly slips out of his own smock and hands it over as well. In this heat, it's more relief than sacrifice. A t-shirt is more than enough.

Hattie and the cadet I don't know approach the girls quickly, but Phillie hangs back, looking rather freaked out. I pull out my phone and check it again. Nothing. I mutter a rude word under my breath, and move back to the bottom of the ramp, so I won't be bellowing near the girls.

"I need someone to run back to the minibus, radio for help, and get Iqbal—Isaar, that is—here ASAP," I shout to the others. "It's straight back to where we met this young man and his pony, then all the way along the path to the main road. Carry your phone in your hand and keep checking the signal. If you get one, call 999 immediately. Who's the fastest runner?"

Though his tanned skin still looks unnaturally pale, the gypsy-boy gives a slight snort, dashes down the ramp, clears the tyre marks in two leaps, and bounds off up the slope like a deer. After a few moments, we hear the sound of hooves on dry earth. Who's the fastest runner? The pony. Silly Sam.

"Okay, so I want the three fastest to run in three different directions and don't stop until you get a signal or find a landline. Soon as you do, call 999. Just in case that pony puts its foot down a rabbit hole." Far better this be called in four times than not at all. I'm no doctor, but those girls clearly need urgent medical attention.

"Sam?" It's Phillie. "We've cut them loose, should we move them out of there?"

I hurry back up the ramp and look again at the girls. The smocks cover them like blankets, now. First aid instructions run through my head. Don't move the casualty... But it's really hot in there... For a moment indecision grips me. But they've been in there for hours, a few minutes more is better than risking hurting them if they've got internal injuries or broken bones, surely?

"Don't move them until Isaar comes," I say. "Don't give them any water yet, either." They might need rushing straight to an operating theatre, for all I can tell. "Check under them for grenades, though. Without lifting them, obviously. But I think they'd be telling us if there was anything like that."

Hattie and Phillie and... Angela seems to be the name... shoot me horrified looks, but begin to query the girls gently about whether they're lying on anything hard and knobbly. The answer is in the negative, so they slip a hand underneath anyway, to check, then shake their heads at me.

"Thank God!" says Henry.

"Well, it seemed unlikely," I say. "But better to make sure. Wait a minute..." I tense, listening. "There's a vehicle coming..." Should we all run into the woods? Try to take the girls with us? So much for not moving them...

Then I get a glimpse through the trees. A familiar white minibus. Someone's decided that minor things like actual minibus driving licenses are not important at a time like this.

I'm pretty sure it's Rish at the wheel when he revs up the engine and drives straight at the locked gate. It flies open with a *crunch-crash*. I run down the ramp, waving him into the part of the clearing furthest from the tyre tracks.

Isaar's jumping out before the minibus has even stopped, the first aid kit in his hand. Whenever someone gets hurt on exercise everyone shouts *"Isaar."* One of the perils of studying medicine. It's lucky he's with us today, though.

"Where are they?" he asks, wide-eyed.

"In the horsebox. Come on..."

Isaar hurries towards the girls the moment he sees them, drawn to their pitiful state like a moth to a flame, but as soon as they notice *him* they recoil in terror and start trying to drag themselves away, sobbing and... wailing. They're so afraid. Isaar stops dead, looking stricken.

"No, no, it's okay," Hattie says, in a tone of dismay. "That's, uh... that's Doctor Iqbal. He's an army doctor... he's here to look after you. There's no need to be frightened..."

But it's no good. Isaar crouches and shuffles closer in as un-looming a manner as possible, but the girls keep trying to get away, fighting Hattie and the other two when they try to restrain them. They're becoming hysterical.

I touch Isaar's arm. "Come on," I mutter.

He gets up and follows me out. I can see him shaking, and

his breathing isn't quite steady. I give his shoulder a quick squeeze.

"Right," he says, his voice almost normal. "Hattie, Phillie, tip a bottle of water over each of their heads, straight away, and start giving them little sips. Not too much. It's like an oven in there. They feel hot, right?"

Hattie puts a hand on one of the girls' foreheads. "They're burning up."

"Heat exhaustion, probably heat stroke. They've clearly been there for hours."

"I was afraid to give them water," I say. "I thought they might need an operation."

Isaar shrugs. "Fasting before an operation is preferable but not essential. They need the water more." He raises his voice slightly, again. "Hattie, the sooner we get them out of here and into some shade the better. You'll need to get them uncovered and wet them down all over—we've got to lower their body temperature. But first I need you to examine them for me, check for internal injuries or breaks. Don't worry, I'll talk you through it."

"Right," says Hattie, looking a bit unnerved by this responsibility.

JASPER

When I trot back into the clearing, the officer guy is just marking off an area under the trees.

"This is a female-only zone, okay?" he's telling everyone. "Nobody comes near here. *Right?* Now everyone get on the other side of those vehicles and turn your backs. *Don't walk across the clearing!*" He's still trying to preserve as much evidence as possible.

I'm not female, so presumably these orders apply to me too. I head a little way up into the forest and watch from there as the three female soldiers carry the poor girls out to that shady area. I peep for just long enough to make sure they're doing the right thing—uncovering them and wetting them and fanning

47

them to cool them—then I don't look again. That Iqbal fellow who the officer wanted fetching clearly knows what's he's doing.

There's nothing to do now but wait. And think. Which I'd rather not. I lean forward and wrap my arms around Molly's warm neck, hugging her. I can hardly believe what's happened, what I've seen. Those poor girls, it makes me feel sick to think about them.

My head feels like it's being stretched to exploding point. *How—why*—would anyone—*could* anyone—do something like that?

SAM

Isaar's retreated behind one of the white vans, within earshot of the girls but well out of sight. He's got his forearms pressed to the van side and his forehead rammed up against his knuckles. His bowed shoulders are shaking.

I take an uncertain step towards him, but even as I do he straightens, squares his shoulders and lifts his hands in prayer. Right. God will comfort him better than I can. I mean, what was I going to say, anyway?

It's all right? It's not.

The girls will be fine now? Who knows if they will be?

At least the girls are free? How long until they'll really be free, inside?

Now there're some clues, they'll find the other girls? If they find them from one set of tyre tracks—in time—I'll eat my beret.

No, right now, I'd be no help at comforting anyone. I suppose all I can come up with is, *well, at least they're not dead.* Only right now, maybe they wish they were.

This is no good. I head for the minibus, where Rish is kneeling at the front with the radio next to him. The plastic bumper and front grill have shattered and fallen off, and he seems to be trying to push a big dent out of the metalwork with his bare hands.

"Did you get through to Sergeant-Major Wood before

coming here?"

"Isaar radioed him as we were driving. We phoned 999 first, of course, and radioed HQ as well. Though don't ask me where the blinking ambulance has got to." His hand slips and he mutters something suspiciously like a swearword.

Taking his hand out from under the bonnet, he makes to put a bleeding finger in his mouth, sees all the grime, and fishes out a piece of tissue instead. Wraps the wound, then just kneels there, staring at the dent in a way that suggests he's only half seeing it.

The tissue is going red pretty fast. Well, this will cheer Isaar up, having a patient he can actually touch. I glance around... Isaar's still praying. But not formal prayers—the only time he'll ignore you. Nothing I've read and nothing they've said has really convinced me Islam is quite as peaceful as they so passionately believe—but I've nothing but respect for them, and those like them.

"Isaar, Rish's bleeding," I call.

"I'm fine." Rish gets to his feet, but by the time he's walked along the side of the bus and deposited the radio in the back, Isaar is there.

"*Are* you bleeding, Rish?"

Rish doesn't even attempt to lie to his twin. "Just a little."

Isaar sighs and goes to fetch some things from the first aid kit. I can hear him calling soft inquiries to Hattie, checking on the girls.

The girls... When he comes back and briskly deals with the bleeding finger, I sit down beside Rish, feeling rather sick. I can't think about the girls any more right now.

Wait... What's that?

Yes! Finally. A siren.

RUTH

They still haven't brought Sasha back. Daniyah cried for ages. She kept on saying, 'But I checked! I checked her!' They took her away after a while to cook. She asked if she could have

49

some help and when they said yes she chose Becky—the ballerina—along with Kim and Louise, the two year tens. I don't know why. Surely Kim and Louise are the last ones we want the men harassing? I think Louise is only fourteen. But they came back after a while, right as rain, with big trays of sandwiches—which everyone fell on like starving wolves. Gemma and Annabel bullied me until I had some too.

One of the men came after that and made us all sit in rows and recite Arabic. He didn't tell us what it meant, so I just kept my head down and didn't say it. He's finally gone away. They all have. But the hold doors are locked, we've checked.

So now I'm sitting here trying not to think about Yoko. Or Sasha. Or... pretty much anything. Apparently I'm looking pretty much back to normal, because Annabel's huddling up to me instead of putting her arm around me and telling me it's going to be okay. I don't feel normal. I'd like to say I feel numb but I don't. Kind of detached, yes, but anything other than numb.

"What do you think they had us saying?" whispers Annabel eventually.

"Verses from the Quran, probably," says Gemma.

"So... do they think we're Muslim now?"

"I dunno," says Gemma.

"None of it sounded familiar," I say. "I think *those* words would sound familiar. So probably not."

"Why didn't you say it, then?" says Gemma, under her breath.

"Because I'm not sure. I don't speak Arabic, do I?"

"Perhaps Daniyah knows," says Annabel.

"From the way some of the men were mocking her, I don't think her Arabic's too good either," says Gemma. "But I don't know what she was thinking, choosing Kim and Louise as fellow cooks."

The answer comes to me, suddenly. "Perhaps she thinks they might have a chance to escape. Since they're allowed out of the hold."

Gemma is silent for a moment. "Didn't think of that."

"I only just did."

There's a screech as one of the doors is opened. The men shove someone through and slam it again.

It's Sasha.

Her frizzy hair is all over the place, blood and tears streak her face and her clothes are torn. Her pyjama bottoms have disappeared entirely. She half claws, half crawls her way into the corner of the room and curls up there, long, thin sobs raking her. They echo around the hold, which is suddenly so silent you could hear a pin drop onto the metal floor.

"Well, they didn't kill her," says Gemma at last, her voice shaking. "That's good, right?"

SAM

The clearing is swarming with police, ambulance crews and plainclothes officers. I'm not sure where the gypsy-boy has gone. He's probably still watching from somewhere nearby, but he's made himself scarce. Perhaps he's afraid someone will try and make him go to school.

We've debriefed to what feels like every uniform in the clearing about ten times over, and we're all gathered around the minibus, trying to stay out of the way, when Sergeant-Major Wood arrives in the other minibus with the second platoon.

"What the hell happened to your bus?" the Sergeant-Major demands, as soon as he's spoken to whomever's now in charge.

"I drove it into the gate." Rish points apologetically. "I'm sorry."

"Was twenty meters really too far to run?" Wood sounds exasperated.

"It *was* urgent," I say.

"Not quite that urgent." Rish, honest as ever. "I was just so angry, I took it out on the gate. And the bus, unfortunately."

"There goes your pay for the next few months," smirks Will. The mood has lightened a bit, now the experts are here; now that they've confirmed the girls will be fine—at least physically.

"The next year, more like," says someone else.

"Perhaps Isaar should buy you a stress ball for Christmas," calls Hattie, from inside the bus, just a hint of hysteria in her light heartedness. "Might be cheaper for you! Oh... well, for Ramadan, or whatever..."

"Perhaps I should just keep my temper better," says Rish sourly.

"I think in the circumstances, we'll just quietly forget about it," says Sergeant-Major Wood, "what with your complete absence of *minibus license*, Iqbal."

"I'm not apologizing for *driving* the thing!"

"Nor should you, but I dread to think of the paperwork, so it didn't happen, okay? Right, you've done a really good job here, everyone, so *very well done*. We're free to go now, so mount up, and let's get back to the city of dreaming spires."

Once we're all aboard and driving along, I fish my phone out and check the news. People are chattering and even laughing, now. I try to feel more positive. After all, two of the girls *are* free, and *we* found them. The ambulance crew reckoned they wouldn't have lasted much longer—that we probably saved their lives. But I just can't stop seeing them, lying there, tied up...

Then a headline catches my eye. "Hey, listen to this: 'M4 girls—Doctors confirm no life-threatening injuries!'"

"What?" asks Isaar, grabbing my phone.

I wait for the clamour of similar questions to die down. "It sounds like they're going to be okay, right, Isaar?"

"Cuts, bruises, some need skin grafts..." mutters Isaar, as he reads. "Some broken bones, and a couple of concussions. One girl in an induced coma but it's precautionary. Well, that's about as good as anyone could hope for."

"Hey, go to Twitter," says Phillie from the back. "Someone's started a campaign."

"To do what?" someone asks.

"Well... put pressure on the government to get the girls back, I suppose."

"That's redundant," snorts Will. "Any government with the

slightest pretension to re-election will be busting its collective gut to get those girls back in one piece."

When I get my phone back from Isaar, I see what Phillie's talking about as soon as I look at my Twitter feed. People are tweeting pics of themselves holding up signs saying #GetOurGirlsBack. Hattie and the other two are already ripping a page out of an A4 notebook. Soon the sign is travelling around the bus.

"Say cheese, Sam," says Rish.

"This is hardly a smiling matter."

"No, it's not. Well, I got you looking grim as." He hands my phone back to me and takes the sign from my hands. "Now do me. Here's my phone."

I don't accept it. "I don't think that's such a good idea, Rish, not in your uniform."

"Especially in the uniform. That's why you're all taking pics now, isn't it?"

"Muslims in the army..."

"It's not *so* unusual for Muslims to be in the army these days, Sam," says Isaar. "Not after all the stuff that's been going on. Loads have joined up in the last few years."

"Yeah, and it's not that uncommon for one to turn up mysteriously dead, either."

"Better a mysterious corpse than a live coward." Rish hands his phone to Isaar instead, holds up the sign, and looks sternly into the camera. Isaar snaps the photo and they swap.

"Well, if extremists show up at the house in the middle of the night, I'll direct them to you," I tell them.

Rish frowns slightly, clearly at the consideration that they might be endangering me as well as themselves.

"Oh for goodness' sake!" I say. "You aren't not posting them because of *me*."

"You say that, yet try to stop *us?*" points out Isaar. "From doing this *one tiny thing* we can actually do?"

I groan. He's right.

The sign is passed on to the row in front, and there's a brief silence as everyone tweets their pics, then a lot of banter as they come up on everyone's feed. Inevitably, it's not long after that before the discussion moves to exactly what we'd like to do with the terrorists if we had them on their own.

I don't join in. It's not that I wouldn't be happy to see the men dead. In fact, the way I feel right now, if you put me in a room with those men, I'm not quite sure what I'd do, and feeling like that frightens me. But most of the suggestions being bandied around are sick and a few definitely shouldn't be being made in front of the girls. Officers and gentlemen, and all that. The girls are well inured to the things guys say when in the presence of honorary guys like Women Officer Cadets, though, and seem thoroughly approving. I s'pose I can see why.

Rish and Isaar stay quiet too. I can see what they're thinking. If we really did these things, rather than just talk about them, we'd be no better than the extremists. *Their* silence is apparently more inflammatory than mine, because it's not long before Will demands, "So what would *you* do with them, Isaar?"

Isaar frowns for a moment, then says into the expectant silence, "Convert them."

There's a roar of—slightly incredulous—laughter.

Will snorts rudely and says, "You'd better convert them to Christianity, then, 'cause Muslims are supposed to kill their enemies, aren't they?"

There's another silence, an embarrassed one this time.

"Muslims are allowed to fight people who attack them." Rish speaks calmly, but he's clearly annoyed. "I believe that's the same for Christians."

"You don't seriously think you could convert those monsters, do you?" Henry jumps in, before Will can say anything else. From the haunted look in his eyes, he's also having trouble feeling quite as happy as everyone else.

Isaar shrugs. "Unfortunately they're not monsters, they're human beings. I agree it would be a lot cleaner and easier if they weren't. And no, I don't think most of them would repent. It's just my preferred option, that's all."

"So what would you do when they won't repent?" persists Will.

54

"We'd kill them," says Rish. Another silence falls, 'cause everyone else was only half serious, but he speaks with real conviction. "Well," Rish adds more lightly, "I imagine I'd have to kill them and Isaar would just provide moral support."

"I'd fight too," Isaar protests. "If it came to that." He looks sick and miserable at the mere thought.

"Doctors shouldn't have to kill people," says Henry firmly, and there's a murmur of agreement from around the bus.

"What about you, Sam?" says Will.

I don't feel like talking at all, right now, but I'm going to have to say it.

"If it was necessary, I'd help Rish, of course."

SASHA

I can't think.

There's nothing in my head but men. And pain.

I'm back in the hold. There are no men here now.

In my head, there are men.

I'm here alone in this corner, like rape is contagious or something...

Rape. That's what it's called, what they did. It's too small a word.

How long have I been in this corner? I want to hide here forever. Don't let them ever come back, please...

Please what? Please God? How can there be one? Always vaguely thought there was, not enough to go to CU or anything but... now I know.

But that means we're alone, in an uncaring world, and there's no hope at all...

Men. Cruel, harsh, dispassionate, stinking... so many.

What do I do?

What if they take me again?

What do I do?

What do I do, what do I do, what do I...

There's someone there! I flinch into the corner, try to press myself through the wall.

It's Ruth. Grey and strange in the odd clothes. She sits down, not too close. Folds her hands on her knees, her eyes closed. She's praying for me, I suppose. It's nice. I don't know why if there's no God, but it is.

The men are still pressing in my mind; my body still quivers with memory. Ruth sits with me, silently. Doesn't tell me I'm okay, or try and get me to say that I am. Just sits there.

Eventually I creep from the cold corner and nestle my way under her arm, like a chick under a mother bird's wing. Hide my face in the folds of her hood. And cry. Cry, cry, cry. Ten times harder than I have yet. She holds me tight and rubs my back, on and on. Says nothing. What could she say?

"There's no God!" I choke at last. "There's no God, Ruth!"

She doesn't reply. Rub, rub, hug, hug. Doesn't think it's time for Theology 101, maybe. But I actually want to know. Want to know why her prayer makes me feel better.

"There's no God, is there? Gemma's right! She's always been right! No God could let this happen!"

"There is a God, Sasha." Her voice is very soft and quivers slightly. Oh. She's crying too. "Who loves you ever so much. And He's so, so sorry that those men treated you like this. And if they don't repent, He will punish them very, very severely. Maybe forever."

I hadn't thought of that. That the men will be punished by God. "How could He let them? If He loves me!"

"Because He has given every single person—you, me, the men, everyone—the right to make their own decisions. To not be His puppets."

"I wish I *was* a puppet! Puppets don't get... don't get..." I'm crying again. Crying and crying.

Someone creeps up and puts something beside us. Daniyah. Looking frightened. But it wasn't her fault. I should tell her, but I can't speak right now. I can only sob...

...Ruth's combing my hair with her fingers. What's left of my hair. Whole hunks of it are gone. But she combs and combs and combs and combs until it's all untangled, then fastens it neatly back in a ponytail. Well... as neatly as my hair can ever be fastened... Then she washes my face and neck and arms, and gently chivvies me into taking the sponge and washing... elsewhere. I'm so sore. I ache so much. But I feel so dirty.

I'm so scared.

Ruth ties that grey scarf around my crazy hair, tucking it all under it. Then pulls the hood over my head. The trailing fabric covers the top of my robe, which is all ripped and gaping, and my pyjama top, where half the buttons are gone. She helps me put on Daniyah's pashmina, like a sarong, so that the rips in the bottom of the robe don't show my legs. She makes me put her socks on, too, since my shoes are gone—I mustn't, mustn't think about how and when they went, not now when I've almost stopped crying...

"There," she says quietly, "you're all spick and span."

Decent, she means. As the men would have it.

"Will it help?" My voice is so small. "Will it?"

Ruth is silent for a moment. I know whatever comes out of her mouth will be the truth, which isn't as comforting as I'd have thought.

"I don't know," she says.

DANIYA

Sasha's stopped crying at last. Everyone's beginning to relax and talk again.

Becky shifts to sit beside me. "Did you see what I saw, earlier?" she says in a low voice.

"When?"

"On the deck. When we carried the food up to the bridge."

I didn't really see anything other than deck and sea. I was concentrating so hard on getting up the ladder-like staircases in the long robes while holding a tray, with the ship going up and down on the waves, but I suppose Becky has great balance. "What?"

She lowers her voice even more. "There's an inflatable life raft in a box on the wall. All we've got to do is get out there, throw it into the sea and jump in after."

"Jump overboard?" It'd crossed my mind earlier, but I was sure we'd drown before reaching shore. But with a raft...

"I wish *someone* had a watch," says Becky. "I can't stand not knowing the time. But it must be going dark soon, even at this time of year. I'm sure we had lunch very late. It would be better to try and get away when it's a little darker, obviously. We'll be smaller targets."

My mouth goes dry and my heart thuds in my chest. Targets. What if we get shot? *Allah... I'm so scared...*

But... I can't help glancing at Sasha, still coiled around Ruth. 'Honourable marriage' will only mean one man at a time, but apart from that it's going to be no different. Anyway, because I chose Kim and Louise as cooks they're being paraded under the noses of the men and they're only fourteen and fifteen. This is why I chose them and if I bottle out, I'll have put them in danger for nothing.

Suddenly I can't wait for the men to come and get Becky, Kim, Louise and me again. I can't seem to take my gaze from the floor, though—I don't want to look at the others. Becky hasn't mentioned anything about them going too. I mean, there's an armed man outside the hold. In a film they'd manage it, but I just can't see how. It's the four of us or no one.

Finally the door squeaks again. "Cooks," yells one of the men.

We get up and follow him out, keeping our eyes down. He leads us to the kitchen as before. Big bags of pasta wait for us, and meat and cheese. This will be much more of a test of our cooking skills.

We try our best. It'll matter if we don't get away. I murmur the plan to Kim and Becky murmurs it to Louise as we work, interspersed with actual cooking instructions—the man is lounging just outside the kitchen door. Finally we're ready. We've loaded one tray with a big dish of pasta and a bowl full of hunks of bread, a second with crockery and cutlery, a third with glasses and a jug of water, and the fourth with fruit.

We look demure and nicely encumbered. Good.

BECKY

My heart is pounding so hard it's hurting me, so hard I'm almost afraid the man will notice. We head for the bridge, like at lunch time, and the man follows on behind. Struggling up all the flights of stairs, we're desperate to hitch our robes up, but Daniyah's impressed upon us that we must under no circumstance show our ankles, so we can't.

There... sky ahead. It's fairly dark, too. This is the deck with the raft. My heart is pounding, pounding... This is our chance. My chance. My second chance, after I wasted the first... Kim, Louise and Daniyah step through the door ahead of me—I follow. They've already placed their trays silently on the deck and are hauling the door shut. The man sees what we're doing... springs forward.... I drop my tray—no, too loud!—and throw my weight against the door as well. It thuds into its housing; we spin the lever... locked.

Quick, quick, before he finds another way out... Someone may have heard that crash...

"Where's the raft?" Daniyah's voice is thin with fear.

"There!" gasps Louise, sounding wildly excited, even as I grab at the box.

It's a lot heavier than I expected. We wrestle with it for a moment, then realize we're supposed to open the box and remove the raft from inside it. We're taking too long! I look along the deck... another door stands open, oh no, any moment...

"I'll get the door!" I let go of the raft and sprint across the damp metal deck... I'm almost there when I tread on my hem... *slam*... all my breath is gone in a solid smack of pain. I struggle up onto my knees—I can hardly move, can't control my heaving, whooping chest, but I've got to get to that door, got to...

I'm half way to my feet... I'm on my feet... I lurch forward, reach for the heavy metal thing...

It smashes into me as the man slams through it... *snap*... pain sears through my arm and I stagger back against the wall behind the door. The man's rushing on towards where the others are teetering over the rail, hasn't even noticed me, grey in the dark.

I must get to the side of the boat, get overboard...

I've still got a chance.

DANIYAH

"Let's climb over first," I say, once we've got the pack of heavy orange plastic to the rail. "We want it to land with us..."

Balancing the raft on the rail, we scramble up. My foot catches in the hem of my robe and I almost pitch headfirst into the sea... Almost there, almost there, we're going to do it... Where's Becky? I glance around...

There's the man, pounding across the deck...

"Go!" I scream. Kim and Louise disappear from beside me, I yank on the raft, toppling it after them, and jump...

There's a tremendous yank around my chest and arms and I'm hanging there... my robe must be caught... I wriggle frantically, flailing, but I'm helpless. Oh no, I'm rising back towards the rail! I look up... the man has hold of my robe and he's hauling me up.

I'm panicking, now, gasping for breath, I twist and turn, trying to slip out of the robe and let myself fall. The robe goes up over my head, I'm almost free... *ow*... no... The robe's caught on the hood—or he's got hold of the hood now—and the hood is cutting into my chin, all my weight on it... *ow ow ow... can't breathe...*

The rail scrapes against my back—I struggle with the fabric, I've got to get free, I've got to... I can't see anything... *I've got to...* then I'm slamming down on the deck and it's too late, I'm caught, oh *Allah, Allah help me*, I'm *caught*...

"Traitorous bitch!" something slams into my side, hard. My mind insists on telling me it's a foot or a rifle butt but it doesn't matter, it really, really hurts. My robes are still up around my head—so's my pyjama top, I can feel the cold deck against my back. I fight to free my hands from the fabric and cover myself...

"You are no *Muslimah*!" the man is shouting. I can hear doors squeaking and slamming, running footsteps. "You are a filthy treacherous whore!"

I finally free a hand and get the fabric down over me and out of my eyes. He steps forward... the way he's looking at me... I shrink back and, panicking, start to recite the Islamic creed. "*La ilaha illa'llah...*" I whisper. *There is no God but God...*

He stops, his angry eyes burning into mine; hastily I drop my gaze and carry on reciting, "*Muhammadun rasul Allah...*"

His voice comes again, harsh and unappeased: "The court will deal with *you.*" A blur of movement... pain explodes across the side of my head... darkness spirals in around... consumes me...

BECKY

Daniyah crumples to the deck, blood already gleaming wetly on her brow where the rifle butt struck her and I'm frozen against the wall, shaking... I've got to try and reach the rail, but there are more men, now, and my head is swimming with pain, though I'm cradling my arm as carefully as I can. I'll just... I'll just run and jump. Like Ally jumped out of the horsebox. Pretend I'm doing a fish dive and tip myself headfirst over the rail...

What if I drown? My arm's broken...

But the raft's there, somewhere...

But what if they see me? What if they shoot me?

If you stay here, they'll see you anyway. I tell myself that as sternly as I can. I'm going to run. Three. Two. One. *Go, Becky!* I lurch from behind the door, stagger forward... straight into the grasp of the leader as he steps through onto the deck. *No!*

"What's going on?" he demands—I try to twist free and he shakes me until my vision starts greying out.

"The cooks are trying to escape," says the man who just hit Daniyah. "We caught one... if you've got one, only two got overboard."

"*Only* two?" snarls the leader. "If they got a good look at the ship..."

"The ship's name was covered when we brought them on board," says the man quickly. Placatingly. "No one's going to be able to figure out which vessel they came off."

"You'd better hope you're right."

"What shall we do with that one?" asks one of the other men.

Oh no, he's talking about me...

The leader gives me such a powerful shove I reel all the way across the deck and trip over Daniyah's unconscious body, sprawl beside her. I land on my broken arm and the pain overwhelms me. I vomit, just missing Daniyah.

"What use is a disobedient wife?" I hear the leader dimly, through the fog. "She's a slave too."

Footsteps approach—hands grip my pyjama bottoms, yank them down.

"No!" I yell. "No, *please*...!" I twist onto my back, my good arm ready to push him away. He's put his rifle aside; he's reaching for his fly... The other men are there, I can't go for the gun, not swamped in fabric with my PJs round my ankles. I don't know what to do... How can I stop them?

"Stop!" I cry. "*Please, stop.* I..." Inspiration strikes... "It's... it's my time of the month!" It's a lie, and my cheeks burn to mention the subject, but surely they won't want to... "It's my time of the month, do you understand? Please, do you understand?"

The man kicks me—pain explodes through my stomach, but he's straightening, fastening his trousers, stepping away... relief floods through me.

Then I realize he's picking up the rifle, cocking it.

All I can do is scream.

LOUISE

I flinch as the sound of a shot echoes from the ship, and try to hunch lower in the water, but a wave laps into my face, salt water stinging my eyes.

"Kim?" I call softly, terrified the men will hear me, although the ship has already moved some distance. "Kim? Becky? Daniyah? Where are you?"

"Louise?"

I try to swim in that direction, the loose robe dragging in the water, the fabric of the hood weighing down my arms. "Kim?"

"Louise!"

"Kim? Have you got the raft?"

"Yes! Yes, I'm here, I've got it... I don't know how to make it inflate..."

There... I glimpse something orange in the twilight, and struggle on towards it. "Don't inflate it yet! It will show up way more than us!"

A few more dragging strokes, and I'm beside her, grabbing onto the un-inflated raft. I can't help looking back at the ship again. One bullet through the raft and they can just sail off and leave us to drown...

But the ship's even further away, now, and there's no sign it's planning to turn around.

"*Daniyah?*" I call. "*Becky?*" Silence. Well, lapping waves against the raft, but other than that, silence.

"I'm not sure they managed to jump," says Kim in a small voice. "I only caught a glimpse, but I think I saw Daniyah being dragged back over the rail. And I only heard one other splash and that would be you."

I didn't hear Becky hit the water either. My stomach tightens at the thought of that plunge from the ship—the furthest I've ever fallen in my life. The water felt anything but soft; I can still feel the sting from the landing. But the thought of still being on the ship makes my stomach tighten even more. Has one of the others been shot?

We float in silence until we can hardly see the ship any more, then we examine the raft as best we can in the growing darkness.

"I think we just keep pulling on this," I say. "Watch out..."

I pull and pull as hard as I can, but the yellow cord just keeps coming, and coming... My heart sinks... it's broken; it's never going to operate... but then there's a resistance... "Yes, here goes!" I yank again. I'm expecting an explosive whoosh, but the raft just writhes sluggishly in the water and slowly, painfully slowly, unfolds and expands.

"Well, that was an anti-climax," says Kim, her voice shaking with cold and nerves.

"Yeah," I agree, feeling for the opening that will let us get inside. "At least it's gone up, though. I really didn't think about it before, but it looked rather old, didn't it?"

"Don't say that, Louise! I'll be scared it's going to sink."

"Here's the door!" My teeth are chattering now. It may be summer but we're out in the deep ocean and the water's really cold.

It's not easy getting up into the raft, but with Kim hanging on with one hand and giving me a shove with the other, I finally manage to tip myself over the edge. Dragging her in after me is easier.

"Come on, let's do the flap up," says Kim, shivering.

"Hang on, let's check what we've got first. There should be survival stuff in here, right? Maybe a transmitter of some kind?"

"I suppose," concedes Kim. "I don't know."

"Yes," I say firmly. "There should be water, and food, and a transmitter, and a torch and maybe fish hooks and stuff like that."

"Fish hooks? In an inflatable boat? You've got to be kidding!"

"Well, maybe not fish hooks, but you get the idea. Help me look before it's completely dark."

We feel our way over the entire of the interior of our little raft, and even trace our hands over the tarpaulin roof that keeps out the elements. But there's nothing.

"But there has to be!" I say. "I'm sure life rafts are supposed to have stuff like that!"

Kim is silent for a while. "Well, you said it yourself," she says at last. "It looked like a really old one."

It's almost pitch black by now. We zip up the door flap and huddle together for warmth.

"We'll look again tomorrow," I say. "We must have missed it. We probably won't need it, anyway. I mean, a ship's bound to pick us up as soon as it's light, right?"

JAMES

Everyone's gone home now except for Kessie, and Kessie's mum is in the kitchen with Mama, washing up after John and my birthday party. We're seven today. Kessie is still six, so we feel very grown-up.

"What do you think happened to those chocolate mousses?" says John.

"There were only four of them, I expect they're still in the fridge. I'll see if we can have them now." I head out into the hall.

"The Ministry of Defence have confirmed that the two schoolgirls were found by a group of Oxford University Officer Cadets but declined to comment further..." The TV is on in the kitchen, still showing news about those kidnapped girls that we prayed for in assembly this morning. It's good that they've found two, though Mama said that the men hadn't been very nice to them. Still, it's something to be happy about, right?

But when I reach the kitchen, Kessie's mum is standing there with her hands to her face, crying, and Mama is hugging her.

I peep from behind the door for a moment, my stomach churning. I've never seen a grown-up cry before. I don't like it at all. Pretty soon I tiptoe away again.

"No chocolate mousse?" Kessie looks disappointed.

"I didn't ask. Your mum's *crying* in there."

Kessie looks glum. "Oh. Yeah. She does that a lot at the moment."

"Your big sister didn't go to that school, though, did she?"

"No, 'course not. It's just that she has too many hormoyes at the moment."

"Too many what?"

"Hormoyes. When grown-ups have too many it makes them cry," says Kessie knowledgeably.

"Really?" John wrinkles up his nose. "*Kids* cry when they're upset, or when they've hurt themselves. Grown-ups are so weird."

Kessie and I nod in agreement. Hormoyes. I wonder what they are, but Kessie's already talking again. "Well, she has too many because you know she's having a baby, right? Anyway, she was crying before we went to school, *and* after we got home. Because she thinks some of those girls are going to be murdered horribly and that doesn't mix well with the hormoyes that she has too many of."

"Why would they be murdered?" I ask.

"Because they're Christians," says Kessie. "If they refuse to stop being Christians, they'll be killed."

"But you can't make someone stop being a Christian!" objects John.

"Those men who took them away will," says Kessie. I can see she's loving knowing more about this than us. "I asked Mummy what they'll do to them if they refuse, but she wouldn't tell me. So my brother showed me a video online. It was yucky." She looks around and spots her mother's bag. "Look, I'll show you!"

She fishes out her mum's phone and wakes it up.

"Should you be doing that?" I can't help saying.

"Well, we won't find anything on your computer; your mum's got the parent settings cranked up, hasn't she? Let's see, Keith googled 'Christian exec... exec...'"

"Execution?" suggests John.

"That's it. How do I spell it?"

"Um... e, x, e, c, u... um..."

"Ah, got it. Yeah, I think we watched this one. Look."

I'm really not sure I want to watch anything with 'execution' in the title and John also looks doubtful.

Kessie pulls a face at us. "Oh, come on, you two! I thought you were so grown-up, now. I bet you're the only ones at school who haven't seen one of these videos."

"So," says John defiantly. "Perhaps we don't want to see one!"

"John and James are baby chickens! John and James are baby chickens!" sings Kessie, flapping her elbows like wings and clucking at us. "Honestly, you two, it's not much different than one of Keith's computer games!"

"Fine!" John's brown skin has darkened with embarrassment and annoyance, and I can feel my face burning too. "Let's see it, then."

Reluctantly, I turn my attention to the screen. There's a man with brown skin and dark hair like John and Mama and me, kneeling with his hands tied behind his back. Similarlooking men are standing around him with guns, shouting at him in a foreign language. He looks really scared, but he keeps shaking his head and whispering "Jesus..." and something I can't understand, but I think he's saying "Jesus, help me."

They keep shouting at him, and pushing him, and hitting him for a while, then one of them draws a huge knife and yanks the man's head back, and he's whispering, "Jesus, Jesus, Jesus!" and the bad man drives the knife in and...

I'm halfway up the stairs before I realize that I'm screaming. I dive onto my bed and pull the pillows over my head as the sobs start. Dimly I can hear John yelling at Kessie: "...wasn't like a video game, it was *real!* How could you..." and Kessie's wail of protest, but I'm too busy crying to pay much attention. My chest is knotted up in pain and all I can see is that bad man, chopping that poor Christian's head right off...

I writhe from side to side, trying to shake the image out of my brain, but it feels like it's burned in. Like I'll never, ever be free of it...

JOHN
"What's going on?" Mama dashes in. "Where's James? What's happened?"

"Ask Kessie!" I rush up the stairs after James, ignoring

Kessie's snivelling.

I want to dive under a pillow and cry too, but somehow I manage to choke the sobs back and hug my twin. "It's okay, James," I whisper. "It's..." I can't say the word again. It's no good; tears are running down my cheeks...

"Boys, whatever is going on?" Mama's hurrying into the room. "Kessie's crying because you shouted at her, and... oh my, *you're* both crying too..." She peels James out from under the pillows and gathers us in her arms. "Hey, now, shhhh, what's the matter, now? Whatever's the matter?"

"Kessie showed us a video," I manage to sniff. "Of what bad men like the ones who took the girls do to Christians."

I feel Mama catch her breath. "Was there... violence?"

"They cut the man's head off!" sobs James, sounding like he can hardly talk. "And it was real, so he must be *dead*..."

I nod, my face still pressed up against Mama. "He was praying and praying, but they just cut his head right off and plonked it down on his body and cheered and played music like... like something good had happened!" I'm sobbing properly now; I can't help it.

"Oh, boys." Mama hugs us tightly. "You shouldn't have watched that."

"I wish we hadn't," I sniff, "but she called us chicken."

Mama sighs. "I see." She holds us in silence for a while, rubbing our backs and stroking our hair, until we calm down a bit, then she plants a kiss on each of our foreheads and says, "I think I need to go and have a little word with Kessie and her mum." She eases up from the bed and heads determinedly for the door, leaving James and I to hold onto each other.

We remain lost in misery until raised voices reach us. Are Mama and Kessie's mum having a row? But by the time we've dried our eyes properly and crept to the top of the stairs, Kessie's mum is standing in the hall with her coat on, and they're hugging.

Mama spots us, of course. "Ah, boys, Kessie's going home now. Come and say goodbye."

We head downstairs reluctantly, because Kessie will

probably know we've been crying. But Kessie's standing behind her mum, not looking at us.

"I think Kessie has something to say to you," says Kessie's mum, sounding stern.

Kessie almost-looks at us. "Sorry I made you watch that video on your birthday," she says. She shoots a look at her mum and adds hastily, "Or at all..."

James doesn't quite look at her, as he mutters, "S'okay. We shouldn't have watched it."

I make noises of agreement, and the grown-ups seem satisfied.

"Bye, Kessie," says James.

"Bye, Kessie," I say.

"Bye," mumbles Kessie, as her mum walks her out the door.

"Well, I definitely think it's time for bed," says Mama, as soon as they've gone. "Go and get ready, now."

Once we're tucked under the covers, she comes and sits on the edge of James's bed and looks at us both. "Now, try not to think too much about that video, okay?" she tells us. "I know that will be difficult, but just remember the man is a martyr and he's with the Lord in heaven, and if ever, God forbid, it should come to it, I hope you will follow in his footsteps. Now, let's pray to your guardian angels to keep any bad dreams away."

As we pray, I can't help peeping at James, and I don't need to catch the look he shoots me back to know what he's thinking. What we're both thinking.

That poor man was horribly, brutally murdered.

Did Mama really just say that's what she wants to happen to *us?*

JAMES

"Are you two okay?" Mama asks, shutting the door behind us when we get back from school the next day.

"Fine," says John, sounding almost convincing. I keep my mouth shut. No need for us both to lie.

"Hmm," says Mama, and disappears into the kitchen.

We walk through into the lounge and dump our bags, then look at each other.

"We need to figure this out," says John. And although we haven't said a word about it all day—or at all—I know exactly what he's talking about. That would give Kessie a thrill, if she was here. She likes to think it's psychic or something, because we're identical twins. God knows, I certainly don't.

"She can't have meant it how it sounded," I say. "We know how much she loves us."

"Or we're not understanding it right," says John.

"Well, let's find out." I go to the shelf and reach for my child's Bible, but then my hand goes to Mama's grown-up Bible instead. I lift it down and sit beside John on the sofa.

"Mama's Bible?"

"This is *serious*."

"*Proper* Bible serious. You're right."

We rest it across our knees, unopened, and put our hands together. "Dear Lord," I say, "Please explain this to us because we know our Mama loves us loads and we don't understand why she would want us to die."

"Especially not in such a horrible, horrible way," says John. "We are very, very puzzled. So please make it clear. With not too many difficult words. Thank you. Amen."

"Amen." We open the Bible and peer at the page.

"What did we get?"

I try to spell the name of the book. "Mass... Mass... ah... bee?"

John looks blank. "Never even heard of it." He peers as well. "Um, maybe it's Mac, like a Scottish name..."

"But there's two c's..."

"Maccabees." Mama's voice comes from the doorway. "It's the book of Maccabees."

"Oh, I've heard of that," says John. "There's lots of battles and stuff."

Mama comes and lifts the Bible and sits between us, slipping an arm around each of us. "Oh boys, I'm sorry. I didn't mean to upset you. That was a silly thing to say without making sure you understood."

"It's okay." I tap the Bible. "We asked God to explain."

"Well, then. I'm sure He can do it better than I can. Maccabees seven, by any chance? John, do you want to start?"

"Maccabees chapter seven," John reads. "It happened that seven brothers and their mother were arrested and were being com... compelled by the king, under torture..."

It's about a family, Mama explains, when John finishes the first paragraph, who are being forced to deny their faith, just like the man in the video. I read the next paragraph, stumbling over the words as I realize the hideous tortures being described. Then John reads again, and we go on taking it in turns. Each of the first six brothers refuses to deny their faith, just like the man. And each is martyred. Just like the man...

The words of the second brother to the evil king particularly strike me. "You accursed wretch," John reads, "you dismiss us from this present life, but the King of the universe will raise us up to an everlasting renewal of life, because we have died for His laws."

Finally there is one brother left, the youngest one, and the king tries to persuade him to give in, to save himself. I picture a boy our age, nose in the air, ignoring the evil king. So the king tries to get the mother to talk him round. And despite the fact she's just lost six of her children she instead urges him to hold firm. Begs him to!

'My son, have pity on me. I carried you nine months in my womb,' she says to him. And, 'I beg you, my child,' she says. And, 'do not fear this butcher, but prove worthy of your brothers. Accept death, so that in God's mercy I may get you back again with your brothers.'

"Let this be enough, then, about the eating of sacrifices and the extreme tortures." I read the last words of the chapter and Mama blows out a breath in agreement.

"Quite enough," she says. "But... do you understand now?"

I do understand. "You'd rather we held firm, even if it meant we got killed, not because you don't care about us, but because you want us to go to heaven."

"And that's more important than living for years and years," says John.

"My good clever boys," she says, kissing us both. "Exactly. I wish more Christians took this seriously. I suppose they've just never had to think about it."

ANNABEL

I've been doing so much praying this last few days, I hardly recognize myself. I mean, I've always believed in God, been involved in CU and everything, but I can't honestly say I've ever prayed a lot. I've always found it boring. Never come close to how Ruth and Ally pray, like they've got a real relationship with God or something. I've always found the idea of that a bit scary, really.

It's different now. I keep reaching out to Him. And I don't have any epiphanies or anything, but I keep going. I even manage not to break down and cry all the time, and to encourage the others, so I reckon He's there, and He's answering. I told Ruth that—she smiled and said that thing about God bringing good out of bad—I haven't told Gemma, though. I don't want to argue about it. She knows I believe, so nothing's changed there, even if it's starting to feel like everything's changed.

We haven't seen Kim, Louise, Becky or Daniyah for several days. We heard a lot of shouting and running around, a terrible scream, and a shot. Just one. But they haven't brought any of them back. I suppose they tried to get away and they killed them. Sasha took it really badly. Apparently there was something she wanted to tell Daniyah, and hadn't. We keep Sasha away from the men as much as possible. When we do our Arabic recitation, she sits right in the middle, near the back. But a man still comes and takes her out of the hold each night. Only one man at a time, now, which is... something. She struggled the first time and the man beat her so badly, now she just goes with them. Crying and trembling.

There's nothing we can do.

Mostly we've had long speeches about how we're going to make good marriages and be good Muslims—*Muslimah*, they call us. They tell us we have nothing to fear, it will all be honourable and done properly—even that when we get where we're going we'll be married to the men in the 'camp' that we love. But some of the men sneak into the hold at night and harass us. Drag the girls on the outside of the group into the corner and touch them. Hurt them, sometimes. Some of the year thirteens have offered to sit on the outside because they're the oldest. Most of the ones who offered aren't in CU or anything, and I reckon they've had sex already, but it's so brave of them.

We've all been given slips of paper with phonetic Arabic that we're supposed to be learning. The *Shahada,* they call it, the Islamic creed. Apparently when we're chosen as brides we have to say that in front of our new 'husband' to prove we're Muslims. Those are the words Ruth's so worried about. We chant them every day, during the recitation classes and when they make us pray, but she's still keeping her mouth shut. Gemma and I sit in front of her, so the men won't see.

I say the words. I'm ashamed of my weakness, but I say them. And I've learned them by heart, too. I know I shouldn't, but the thought of what happened to Yoko, to Sasha, to the others... I can't face that. Surely God will understand?

LOUISE

I huddle by the entry, watching the breeze whip the flap around. Thank God for the breeze, the sun is so hot today. My mouth is dry and my lips are cracking. Yesterday it rained all day. We were so cold, and we had no way to store the water. We prayed for sun. Now it's sunny and it's too hot. Is God laughing at us? Is He even there?

There weren't any supplies in the raft. None at all. On the second day we finally realized that two pouch things in the walls had water bags in them. There were two others that looked like they should be full too, only they weren't. We've tried not to drink too much, but the last one is almost empty now.

We haven't seen any ships, either. I assumed we were in the English Channel, and there'd be lots of ships, but now I'm wondering if we're in the North Sea, or maybe the Atlantic. Perhaps we're going to drift all the way to America, and they'll find our skeletons in the raft when it gets there and wonder who we are. Kim says maybe we *are* in the English Channel, so we'll see a ship eventually, but it's actually still a really big area of water...

My head jerks up. Ship. I'm supposed to be looking out for a ship, and I've almost nodded off. I scan the horizon again with aching eyes. For a moment I don't notice it, then the tiny silhouette registers.

"Ship!" I yell, lurching to my feet. "Container ship!" My voice cracks painfully. I grab my hood-thing from by my feet and start to wave it, clinging to one of the inflatable roof supports so I don't go overboard. "Kim, ship! We're saved!"

Kim makes it to the doorway and pulls herself up on the other side, pale and unsteady, hood in her hand. Waving like mad, we wait for that little silhouette to turn, to come towards us...

It carries right on across the horizon as minute draws into minute, adrenalin fades, and we grow too tired to keep waving.

"I don't understand," whispers Kim. "Why don't they see us?"

I feel so sick with disappointment that for a few moments I just fight back tears. Finally I try to think it through. My heart sinks. "I suppose... a container ship's really tall, isn't it? So if they're so tall, yet look that small to us, how small do we look to them?"

Kim spits out a couple of rude words, then slumps to her knees and begins to cry.

I crouch beside her quickly. "Stop it, Kim, stop it! Don't waste the water! We've seen a ship, that's great news! Perhaps we're near a... a what-do-you-call-it, a shipping lane. Perhaps there'll be another one, closer. Just don't cry, Kim..."

I can tell she's making some effort to stop, but she carries on shaking and sniffing. My stomach vibrates in sympathy, wanting to join in. I manage to put my arm around her instead. "Let's pray again, Kim, shall we?"

"If there is a God, why's He taunting us with a ship that doesn't stop?" Kim sniffs.

"I don't know!" I feel ready to howl and sob. "I don't know! The only think I know is that it's the *only thing we can do!* So I'm praying! It uses less water than *crying!*"

Kim huddles in the opposite corner for a while, but she's sniffing more in offense now. Before long she slides over to me and we say the 'Our Father' together, over and over. It's easier to keep it up if we take it in turns, so we've put ten knots in a bit of loose thread pulled from the hem of one of our robes to help us keep track—kind of like one of those Catholic rosary-things. We pass it back and forth, saying ten each—in our heads so we don't use up too much water. We watch the horizon as well.

But there are no more ships.

ISAAR

Sam's in the lounge not-watching the telly when we look in.
"We're off now, Sam," I say.

He glances our way, but doesn't quite look at us. "This early?"

"Well, we're going to the mosque first. Then we'll head straight off."

"The mosque. Right. Naturally."

He sounds so bitter, Rish frowns. "Sam..."

"Oh, just go!" snaps Sam.

"It's not...!"

I touch Rish's arm to stop him saying any more. "Sam, do you want to talk?"

"No, I don't want to talk!" He's not even looking at us now.

"Okay." I catch hold of Rish's arm this time, and pull him after me. "See you on Sunday, Sam."

"See you," he mutters.

We shrug our rucksacks on and head out the front door and off along the street, walking in silence for a few moments, until Rish suddenly kicks a stray can clean across the road. "What's Sam's problem all of a sudden?"

"Do I really need to answer that?"

"What, he thinks we're not upset?"

"It was worse for him. He saw more."

"I know, but..."

Sam said very little about anything for three days, before finally, quite suddenly, opening up and telling us about how they found the girls. He talked for about a quarter of an hour, non-stop, then just rushed out of the room. But it obviously did him good to let it out.

If it wasn't for that, I'd rather not know. I can't get it out of my head. *Blood all over their thighs...* I shake my head from side to side, trying to drive the image away. But once the relief of getting it off his chest was over, Sam started getting a bit... funny with us.

"I just can't believe he's blaming *us,*" snaps Rish.

"I don't think he is, Rish. I think he's just... trying to work through everything. I mean, these monsters go around shouting to the world that they're Muslim. Sam's never exactly been a big fan of Islam; how's he supposed to feel?"

"Him and the rest of the world," mutters Rish. But after a moment he adds, "Even if Sam has decided to hate us, I still wish we didn't have to be away this weekend."

"It's Dad's birthday, we haven't much choice. Anyway, I think a couple of days to himself without us popping in and out to the mosque might be just what Sam needs. If he gets too low, he'll go home himself, you know he will. And he doesn't *hate* us, Rish, and he's not going to. Sam's one of the most fair-minded people we know, he'll be okay."

"I love how much faith you have in people, brother," says Rish.

"You think I'm wrong?"

"I certainly hope not."

RISHAD

We walk on in silence, but my heart's definitely lighter after Isaar's words. Fair-minded. Yeah, Sam's fair-minded, all right. Perhaps things will be okay. But he wouldn't be the first non-Muslim friend we've lost, after something like this...

The mosque is a new one, just off the main street that runs near our student let. Mosques are being built all over the place, since the new government got in and pretty much opened the borders. I can't help frowning as we walk. Don't get me wrong, I was all for helping the refugees fleeing from *al-Quabda* and other evil groups, but the government's not being careful enough about who they let come here. *We'll be nice to them, and they'll be nice to us* just doesn't work with extremists.

Our mosque seems to be quiet and spiritual, though. No hint of any...

I look up at the sound of sirens. "What the...!" Police cars are racing up and encircling the mosque. Officers leap out and run inside. "What on earth is going on," I say, rather unnecessarily. It's quite clear what's going on. We've both stopped walking.

Isaar looks horrified. "Please say nothing was planned here!"

The thought makes me feel unclean. I give myself a mental shake. "We didn't know anything about it," I say firmly. "Anyway, they've been following up every lead on pretty much anyone they've got the slightest suspicion about, this week, haven't they? Mosques raided every day. It's just more of the same."

"What do we do now?"

"I suppose we stand and watch for a few minutes, so no one thinks we're rushing away to avoid the police, then we set off home."

Isaar gives me an unsettled look. "*We* haven't done anything."

"*Suspicion* of terrorism offences, Isaar, that's all it takes to

77

have a control order slapped on you. *Suspicion*, not evidence. We'd be out of the university, let alone out of the OTC. We watch."

Isaar sighs. "We watch," he agrees.

ISAAR

Pretty soon I realize that Rish is looking at me, though, not at the mosque. "So, Isaar," he says, when he catches my eye. "We've talked about Sam; how are *you?*"

"I'm fine, Rish," I say quickly.

"Uh-huh. I thought so. You're so fine, you're trying to lie to me."

I fix my eyes on the mosque, wishing we could go in. Because he's right, of course. I am lying. Sam buried himself in silence—I've been trying to bury myself in prayer. And study. With limited success.

"Come on, Isaar," says Rish, his voice cajoling—but firm. "Talk to me."

Normally I'd tell him everything, but this time... this time I can't. But he won't stop until I give him *something*. "I just... It's the way those girls looked at me. As though *I* was the one who had... hurt them. I can't get it out of my head."

"You've been having nightmares." Statement of fact, not a question—after all, he found me crying under my duvet after the worst one. He didn't push me to talk about it right then. But I'm not crying now, and he's going to push.

"Yes, I've had a few. It's not something it's easy to forget, is it? Speaking of which, how are *you*, Rish?"

"You're changing the subject."

Yes, I am, Rish. Because I can't tell you my nightmare. Can't tell you how I dreamt I was the one hurting those poor girls. Can't tell you how in that awful way of dreams, I was unable to stop myself. And I certainly can't tell you how at the end it was just suddenly you and me—and how you looked at me. How you said, "You know what I have to do now, don't you?"

How you raised your rifle and shot me in the head. And woke me.

78

No, I'm never telling you any of that.

TERESA

Thankfully the police cars switch their sirens off once they're in position around the mosque and people can hear my violin again. I can't help glancing that way now and then, though, wondering what's going on. Is it to do with the schoolgirls?

I tried to join the search last week, but they wouldn't take any civilians. I've tweeted a stupid photo of me holding a #GetOurGirlsBack sign, signed a couple of even more useless petitions and donated a day's earnings to some charity that's been set up to look after the girls who escaped. But there's nothing else I can do. The whole thing makes me feel so helpless.

This morning I heard about a prayer vigil tomorrow night, on the Norfolk coast where Yoko Tsumatso's body was found washed up yesterday, and I really want to go, but the train fare is too expensive. I normally busk in Oxford on Saturdays and earn more than in Richford, but it won't be enough.

With a sigh, I play the last few bars of the cheerful piece and change my music. I feel like playing dirges, this week, but no one pays to hear dirges. When I got off the bus this morning, I saw someone spit at a lady in a *hijab*, so I decided to find a spot near a mosque—they must be in particular need of cheering up.

I strike up the next tune, hardly needing to look at the score, but concentrating anyway, trying to make even this jaunty tune a prayer for the girls.

Shouts from the mosque... I glance that way again, just in time to see a white guy with a bushy beard hurl himself over the bonnet of a police car and sprint along the main street. A policewoman and several policemen dash out and tear after him: "Stop, police!"

He ignores their shouts and carries straight on. He's going to pass right beside me, and he's fast, they're not going to catch him, are they? Casually, I turn and place my violin safely on the ground behind me, then step back to my music stand and mess around with the music sheets.

He's only meters away, now.

Wait for it, Teresa, wait for it...

Now! I fling the stand out in front of him—he doesn't even have time to dodge, going head over heels and hitting the pavement with a nasty smack. He's a big guy... I back away, ready to run if he makes it to his feet before... but the police are piling on top of him, dragging his arms round behind his back and handcuffing him.

"Good job," one of the policemen tells me. To my shock, he pulls out his wallet and puts a fifty into my open violin case.

"You don't have to..." I stammer.

"I'll put it on the expenses account," he assures me. "You earned it."

And they're all walking away.

"Infidel bitch!" the prisoner shouts, face contorted with hatred as they pass me. "Whore! You'll burn in hell!"

I turn my face away, hiding a shudder and pick up my music stand, start trying to straighten out the bent bits. I don't quite have the muscles and I'm still struggling with it when a well educated voice says, "Can we help with that?"

I look up: two young Asian men. I do a slight double take... oh, identical twins. Embarrassed, I let them take the stand. They pore over it briefly, then use their superior strength to straighten it out without any apparent discussion over who needs to hold it where.

"Um, ta," I say, as they give it back to me.

They turn to head off. "That was fantastic, by the way," says one.

Oh, they saw... I shrug and give an, *anyone would've done it* smile—they grin and go on their way.

Before I pick up my violin again, I take the fifty pound note from the case and transfer it to my pocket.

I know exactly what I'm going to do with it.

DANIYAH

My head aches so much. I feel so dizzy all the time. Not that there's much reason to move, locked in this tiny, damp, metal room. They empty the toilet bucket and leave some food now and then, and rap on the door to let me know when it's time for prayer, but I may have got totally mixed up and be doing the first prayer of the day at night, for all I know. I've no real idea of the time anymore: there's no light in here. I feel too sick to eat: my head swims and my stomach rejects anything I try to put in it.

Most of the time I just make *dua*. Because if I don't pray, I cry. Well, I still cry, but at least I pray too. Praying stops me from thinking, and thinking is the scariest thing of all. And over and over, I find myself going over my good deeds and my bad deeds, wondering how they balance out... Because there's one thought I just can't keep away.

They're going to kill me. They're going to kill me. They're going to kill me.

Allah, help me. Allah, be merciful...

ISAAR

Rish won't let me drive us home to Bristol. He says I'm too 'mind-locked' as he calls it, with those poor girls. It is so difficult to get them out of my head—studying's been a struggle these last couple of days.

We're home now, though. We head up the drive and before Rish can get his key in the lock the door flies open and Zakirah hurls herself at us. Rish spins her around in his arms and tosses her to me. *Oof!* I spin round too, arms full of happy little nine-year-old. Or not so little, now.

"You've grown again," I pant, carrying her into the house and setting her down in the hall. "You'll be as tall as Feiyaz soon."

Our fifteen-year-old sister is waiting in the hall. Scowling.

She always seems to be scowling, these days.

"It's quite time she put on a headscarf," she sniffs.

That makes Rish scowl too. "Mum and Dad left it completely up to you if you wanted to wear a scarf or not, and Zakirah will get that choice too. Hopefully she'll make a better one than you!"

"It's quite plain in the Holy Quran..."

"Plain as *mud!*" snaps Rish. "You cling to one single *ayah* about which no one can agree when what *is* stated quite plainly is that to be modest we should avoid drawing attention to ourselves. You think that thing on your head fulfils *that?* The veil was a cultural thing that's come to be seen—incorrectly!— as something fundamental to Islam. It's not! The only reason..."

"*Ammi...*" I step forward to hug Mum, relieved at the distraction.

Hijab is a sore topic for both of us since Feiyaz suddenly started wearing a headscarf the other year, and Rish can never stop himself trying to convince her not to. It doesn't help that since 9/11 loads of women have embraced it as a visible sign of their religion. I get it that they want to show that they're not ashamed of their faith, but they've all convinced themselves it's something they *have* to wear to be a proper Muslim...

Zakirah looks unhappy, though the argument is a familiar one by now. I scoop her up again, though she really is too big now.

Rish is hugging Mum too. "Where's *Abbu?*"

"He's gone to the mosque. He thought you weren't going to make it."

"No. We were going to pray in Oxford before we left, but when we got to the mosque the police were busy turning it inside out. We stopped in a lay-by a bit later instead and combined the prayers. Oh, joy. I do so love praying while small boys chuck litter at my head."

"They didn't!" gasps Zakirah, catching my hand and swinging from side to side in excitement. "*Ammi* and *I,* we prayed at home so we'd be sure to be here when you arrived!"

"That's very thoughtful of you," I tell her, earning a big

smile.

"You should always pray at home," mutters Feiyaz. "Going to the mosque like men!"

Even Rish is too used to this grumble to react.

"What happened at the mosque in Oxford?" asked Mum. "No one there actually had anything to do with the kidnapping, did they?"

Rish scowls. "We'd have said not, if you asked us beforehand, but from the way this one guy went sprinting down the road, he was guilty of something."

We've talked the subject to death on the way home and it's clear that the likely stain on the mosque's reputation is the last thing Rish wants to be thinking about now we've arrived. So I'm not surprised when he changes the subject.

"We would have set off sooner, *Ammi*, but we didn't want to leave earlier than necessary when Sam's feeling so down."

Feiyaz is sniffing again, looking like something smelly is under her nose. "It's disgraceful that you're close friends with a non-Muslim. You know it's forbidden."

"Where are you getting this stuff?" demands Rish. "You're worse every time we come home!"

I'm afraid at this rate we'll still be stood in the hall arguing with Feiyaz when Dad gets back, so I give Rish a poke in the ribs with my elbow. "Is there anything we can do, *Ammi?*"

"No, everything's under control. Why don't you spend some time with your sisters? They miss you terribly."

Feiyaz gives a rather less than elegant snort, and makes no objection when Zakirah grabs both our hands and carries us off to her room. She plonks herself in my lap and pours out everything that's happened at school, and at the mosque and in the neighbourhood... It's really good to be with her, but Feiyaz is preying on my mind.

After a while I leave Rish being entertained by a play enacted with Zakirah's favourite toys and slip downstairs.

"However did you escape?" Mum pretends surprise as I enter the kitchen, but I must look serious because her face sobers at once. "What's the matter?"

83

"It's Feiyaz. Maybe it's more obvious to Rish and me because we're not seeing her all the time, but surely you've noticed how extreme her opinions are getting?"

Mum sighs and pushes a hand tiredly through her hair. "Of course we've noticed. We're just not quite sure what to do about it. Your father was talking about cutting off her Wi-Fi, but maybe that would do more harm than good."

I frown. How would I have reacted to something like that a few years back? Or even now. I'd feel persecuted, like I had to stand up for my beliefs twice as hard. "I suppose it might make it worse. But if you go online, extreme interpretations are so dominant. There's so much oil money behind it. That *must* be where she's getting it from. Unless there's someone at the mosque *here*..."

Mum spreads her hands. "Your father's not aware of anyone, and I haven't noticed anything among the women. There's a couple of her friends whose parents have got similar problems, so they may be egging each other on. We're trying to limit how much she sees them without making it clear what we're doing."

I nod. I don't know what else to say. None of us want Feiyaz running off to be a bride to some extremist heretic. "Sure there isn't anything I can do, *Ammi?*"

"With dinner or with Feiyaz?" she says dryly.

"If you can think of anything I can do, just say, but I meant dinner."

"Well, keep trying to talk her round. Rish gets so frustrated, but you... If you can't convince her... Well. Anyway, so far as the meal is concerned, as soon as your father gets home... Ah, there we are..."

We've both heard the door.

I hurry out into the hall to greet Dad, and Rish and Zakirah rush downstairs, and soon we're all sitting down at the table for Dad's birthday meal. Nothing controversial is mentioned, probably because Feiyaz says almost nothing at all, and the atmosphere is relaxed and happy.

My phone buzzes against my leg—so does Rish's. Probably

Sam, he tends to text us simultaneously, rather than assuming we'll magically know what's been said to just one of us, like some people do. My heart lifts slightly. Rish slides his phone out and has a peep. He's not the eldest so he can get away with it better than me.

"Hey, look!" He brings the phone out openly and hands it to me.

The message must have contained a link, because there's a webpage open on screen.

PRAYER VIGIL FOR KIDNAPPED SCHOOLGIRLS

I skim the article quickly. There's a multi-faith prayer vigil being held tomorrow night on the beach where Yoko Tsumatso's body came ashore.

"*Isaar*," says Dad reproachfully. Strictly speaking, there's a 'no phones at the table' rule.

"Sorry, *Abbu*. It's about the schoolgirls. There's going to be a prayer vigil tomorrow night. We should go, Rish. Pray for those poor girls who were violated."

"Not in front of your sister," says Dad quickly.

"I know what it means, *Abbu*," says Zakirah.

"That's why he shouldn't mention it."

I want to say that surely it's better Zakirah know how the world is, but I don't want to seem disrespectful. Mum catches my eye, anyway, so I know she'll talk to Zakirah about it later, if she hasn't already.

"It's on the beach where that Japanese girl's body washed up," says Rish, scanning the article. "Apparently one of the girls who escaped saw her putting her Shinto charms in her pocket as they were leaving the school. The experts think that was quite probably why she was killed. She didn't even speak English and they killed her just because she had a handful of Shinto charms!"

Dad sighs and bows his head, like he feels the shame of what those men have done in the name of Islam pressing on him. I know that feeling.

"If only the rest of them could get away," I say.

"If only they could find them," says Mum.

"I don't see what all the fuss is about," says Feiyaz, speaking at last. "I mean, those girls get to be Muslim now. That's good, right?"

"*Good?*" Rish almost drops his phone in a dish of rice. "What happened to Yoko Tsumatso and those two girls was *good*, was it?"

"Of course it wasn't good. I'm sure that was men acting without orders. Or maybe the girls had been really disobedient..."

"*Disobedient?*" Rish's face has gone so dark I'm afraid he's going to lose it completely. My head's full of those poor girls in the woods too, and I can feel unfamiliar anger trying to creep through my veins.

"Feiyaz," I say quickly. "Just think, *please*. If a load of men dragged you off and told you that you had to become Christian, or Jewish, or Buddhist or whatever, or they'd kill you, and forced you to marry someone you didn't want to marry who ra... did other bad things to you, you'd really think that was *good*, would you?"

"Of course it wouldn't be good. But this is different. They're making them *Muslim*."

"By force!" Rish snaps. "*There shall be no compulsion in religion.* Do you still remember that *ayah?* If they don't convert, they'll kill them!"

"There's no need for them to die. They can just say whatever they're told and preserve their life, can't they? And since it's Islam and it's the truth, they'll come round to it soon enough. What's the problem?"

Rish looks like he if he speaks, he'll explode, so I say, "Other religions have different rules, Feiyaz. *We* may be allowed to say whatever is necessary to preserve our lives, but Christians aren't supposed to lie or deny their faith for *any* reason."

"Exactly." Dad nods. "Isaar's right, Feiyaz. Most of them will probably go along with it—they're only human—but some won't."

"And those are the ones who'll be killed," says Mum. "And they'll probably be the most devout, the very ones Muslims should respect the most. It's all just *awful*. How can you not see that?"

"Look what happened to that poor Japanese girl!" puts in Rish.

Outnumbered, Feiyaz scowls at her plate and says nothing. And suddenly everyone's looking at me. Expecting me to say something that will bring her round. Sometimes I'm afraid my family's expectations will crush me. I never feel like I'm half so good a Muslim as they all think.

"Look... if you've got questions about this, Feiyaz," I venture, "next time you come over to Oxford... well, we've got some really excellent imams and scholars there. Really learned, holy men. I'm sure I could arrange for you to have a chat with one of them. You could ask them anything you're unsure about."

Feiyaz shoots me an angry look, almost hateful. "The fact that *you* recommend them is precisely the opposite of a good reference."

I catch my breath, hurt, despite everything she's been saying recently. Rish does drop his phone in the rice this time, eyes narrowing in rage, but Dad gets there first. "*How can you talk to your brother like that?* I'd trust his opinions on religious matters before anyone in this family—a long way before yours!—maybe even before my own!"

My cheeks burn, it's my turn to look at my plate. Rish glances at me and manages to keep his mouth shut. Even though he agrees with Dad, he knows how much I hate the praise.

"I saw that picture he tweeted this week!" yells Feiyaz. "I was so ashamed! Him in his army uniform! How can you say he's such a good Muslim? All of our brothers and sisters they've killed around the world, and he's *with* them... They're *both* with them!"

"Things are different now, Feiyaz," says Dad. He's angry about the yelling, but he's holding himself in check.

"You think we liked the wars?" snaps Rish, less calmly. "Afghanistan, Iraq? We were on the marches when you were too young to go, trying to stop them! Far too many civilians getting killed, Iraq invaded on trumped up evidence, you think we'd even have joined the University Cadets back then? But that's past history, and *al-Qabda* are the problem now. And if they suddenly told me I had to go and fight them, I'd be proud to go!"

"They can't do that, can they?" Mum looks alarmed.

"Not unless there's a war, Mum," I say quickly. "And they'd be calling everyone up, then."

She lets out a little breath—says firmly, "Now, who wants some more?"

The subject is officially closed. Rish and Feiyaz both stay quiet.

But I can't help looking at Feiyaz and wondering. Wondering how many families have got this problem.

And whether they all know it.

RUTH

Gemma's bullying Annabel into practicing the Islamic profession of faith yet again.

"Gemma, leave her alone."

"She needs to know it. So do you. Have you learnt it yet?"

I pull my knees up, rest my chin on them and say nothing. There's no reasoning with Gemma about this.

She places one of the slips on my knees, just under my nose. "Learn it, Ruth! It may be the difference between life and death. Or have you forgotten Yoko?"

My insides tighten, like they're a rabbit caught in a snare. God knows I haven't forgotten Yoko. I can hardly think about anything else. We managed to clean my dressing gown up a little, but the stains are still there. Sometimes I'm afraid the panic will completely overwhelm me—I know exactly how the rabbit must feel.

In answer to Gemma, I blow the slip off my knees.

She retrieves it quickly. "Careful! Don't let the bastards see you treating that with contempt." When I still don't answer, she glares at me. "Don't you care that they're going to butcher you like an animal?"

Her phrasing brings Yoko's fate back into my mind more clearly than ever. For a moment I can't get a proper breath. My bowels seem to be turning to water. I close my eyes and try to breathe slowly and deeply and calm my body. They march us off to the 'head' in batches several times a day but I don't want to have to bang on the door and ask to go by myself. Kris from year twelve did that yesterday and the guard raped her in the corridor before putting her back in with us. She cried all night. I sat with her for hours but I couldn't get her to eat any breakfast at all. Sasha's with her now—it seems to be doing her good to look after someone else.

Gradually my insides settle down, which is a bit of a miracle because my mind and emotions don't. I know I shouldn't say those words, but I really, really don't want to die. Especially not like a butchered animal.

Lord, St Thomas More said that if we could actually see You, if we could see heaven, then it wouldn't matter what tortures or horrors stood in the way, we would rush straight towards them, without any fear or hesitation...

But I *can't* see God. Not with my eyes. Only with my faith. I'm afraid if it comes to it, I might grab a slip and say those words.

Almost more frightening is the thought that I might not.

GEMMA

I drill Annabel a few more times, then get her to test me.

"I think you're saying it right," she says after a few repetitions, spreading her hands helplessly, "but how should I know?"

"Well, it'll have to do."

Now Daniyah's gone, it's Sasha who knows the most verses of the Quran. Sasha—the dunce in French lessons. Every time we have a recitation class, she listens like she's trying to suck the words into her body through her ears. I reckon she thinks if she can recite them well enough, maybe they'll start treating her like the rest of us again...

Still, it's useful. I can learn them from her afterwards.

Time to have another go at making Ruth see sense. There's no reasoning with her about this. But when I turn to her she's still sitting with her knees up, eyes scrunched closed—and a couple of tears running down her cheeks.

"Ruth?" It comes out more gently than I'd intended. "What's wrong?"

She'd have been justified in laughing in my face at that question, just at the moment, but she doesn't. She just whispers, "I'm so scared."

"Then learn the words." But my voice is still gentle.

"I *can't.*"

"They're just words, Ruth!"

"*Words are more than sounds, falling off an empty tongue...*" She says it so quietly I barely hear.

"What's that supposed to mean?" It sounds vaguely familiar.

"It's from a hymn. I've got it stuck in my head. It's obvious what it means, isn't it?"

"Words *are* just sounds, Ruth. Where does it say in the Bible that you have to die over mere words!"

I've made a mistake. I know that as soon as I see her eyes open, see the intent look that comes onto her face. She's about to recite scripture.

"*Everyone who acknowledges Me before men, I also will acknowledge before My Father who is in heaven; but whoever denies Me before men, I also will deny before My Father who is in heaven.* Jesus said that, Gemma. He also said, *For whoever would save his life will lose it; and whoever loses his life for My sake, he will save it. And, Do not fear those who kill the body but cannot kill the soul; rather fear Him who can destroy both soul and body in hell.*"

"Well, that's nice," I snort. "Your loving God's going to send you to hell if you say a few harmless words to save your life?"

Annabel flinches slightly, but stays silent.

"Not necessarily," says Ruth firmly. "He knows when we've tried our best, and He's very forgiving. But He makes it quite clear what we *should* do. It's not about fear of hell, anyway. It's about loving Him enough and trusting Him enough to overcome our fear of death. *Who shall separate us from the love of Christ? Shall tribulation, or distress, or persecution, or famine, or nakedness, or peril, or the sword?*" Her voice shakes on the last word, but she goes on, "If I bottle out and say it, I know He'll forgive me. But I don't intend to, Gemma, and nothing you say is going to change my mind."

"Then you'll end up dead!" It's all I can do not to yell it. "*Dead.* That means gone. Non-existent. There's no place in the sky where you'll get some big reward for being so stupid. There'll just be no more you. For *nothing.*"

"For everything."

I want to shake the belief out of her, slap her to her senses, hug her for being so brave. "Well, I'm going to survive, do you understand? That's what we should all do. We should say whatever they want us to say, do whatever they want us to do, put up with... whatever we have to put up with, however bad. Because sometime, whether in a day or a week or even a year or ten, we're going to get our chance, and we'll escape, and get our lives back, but we can't do that if we're *dead.* Don't you understand that?"

"It's a good plan," says Ruth gently. "If this life is all you care about."

"This life is all there is!"

"Just now I almost wish I believed that." She thinks about what she said for a moment and finally shakes her head. "No, I don't. Especially just now."

There's no reasoning with her.

I turn back to Annabel. "Sasha taught me the rest of that *ayah*, let's practice that."

Annabel won't look at me, though. "Not right now," she says. Looking at the floor.

91

Argh! Ruth's getting to her, isn't she? "It's your throat," I say deliberately.

DANIYAH

I'm not sure how many days have passed, but my headache isn't so bad now, and I only feel dizzy when I move. I still pray a lot, but I'm thinking too. I can't help it. The man mentioned a court. That means they'll try me for helping Kim and Louise escape. And that means... I have a chance, surely?

I go over the arguments in my head, over and over. *I've always been taught anything under sixteen is too young for marriage, that's why I helped them; I can't help what I was taught. The brave Jihadis have now explained to me that girls can marry from age nine. So I know better now. I would never dream of helping* infidels *again. Let me learn, let me be a good Muslimah... Let me... Let me live...*

Please, I'm just young, just ignorant, I should be educated, not executed... my thoughts always reach this crescendo... *Please?*

Surely they will have pity? *Oh Allah, most merciful and compassionate, let them have pity...*

ALLELUIA

They discharged me from hospital today, and I was able to go home with my parents. Well, we call home wherever we're living at the time. At the moment it's an apartment in East Anglia where they live when they're not on mission, and where I spend the school break. Usually the two coincide a bit.

I'm famous, it seems. For kicking a door open and jumping through it. I've done loads of interviews in the hospital already, and the phone hasn't stopped ringing here since we walked in the door. Mom and Dad are so pleased and proud and relieved. I've left them answering the phone and planning my schedule and come up to my room. Shut the door and sat down on my bed. I feel exhausted.

I'm making the most of all the attention, of course. Turning the focus of every conversation to my Lord and Saviour instead of to me. Anything like this is a great opportunity for evangelization, like Dad always says. He thinks I'm doing great.

But I feel wiped out. Emotionally more than physically. I got off quite lightly when I hit the pavement of the M4. The worst bit is my arm, where a huge piece of skin was ripped off. Almost off. They're still trying to coax it into reattaching, but they say it will probably have to be removed and I'll have to have a skin graft. I wouldn't even dream of complaining, though. They're bringing Zoe out of the induced coma today. They're hopeful, though.

But I can't stop thinking about the others. Especially the others in the horse van. Becky and the others. My friend Becky. Who I left. Can't stop wondering whether I should have stayed with them. Would that have been the more Christ-like action? All I could think about was getting as many of us away as I could. Getting myself away. Should I have stayed?

But what if, as Becky feared, no one else had quite dared to jump if I hadn't gone first? Then no one would have got away...

I just can't bear to think about Megan and Frankie, though, because when I do I wonder if it was because of the escape that they did that to them. And that makes me want to sit down and scream. And scream. And scream.

Is it my fault they hurt them, Lord?
Did I do the right thing? Did I?
Will I ever be able to stop wondering?
Ever?

DANIYAH

I press my ear to the door hinge and listen to the noises echoing through the ship. Is there a boat alongside? There are no portholes and I'm probably below the waterline. My ears may be playing tricks on me. But it sounds almost like... are they welcoming someone?

The coastguard? Oh, let it be the coastguard, let them find us... But it doesn't sound like that. It sounds like someone they're happy to see.

I still haven't been allowed any contact with the others. If I could exchange just a word. Ask someone to tell my family that I love them...

No. No. I've got my arguments ready. They will show mercy. They will... I can't allow myself to think anything else.

Heavy footsteps outside the door... clanking... not a meal time, surely? But the door is opening. My hands fly to my face, checking all my hair is tucked under my scarf.

Two men enter and seize me, march me out. We go along the gloomy ship's corridor... past the door into the hold—I glimpse long lines of black- and grey-clad girls, seated on the floor, but when I turn my head to see them better one of the men snarls and shakes me painfully. Then we're going up some of those steep steps and I'm being hustled into another cabin. "Kneel," comes the order.

I obey, peeping around, my heart pounding... But there's an older, grey-bearded man seated behind a table, who I've never seen before. Other men standing around the walls, as though observing. My trial? Already? I thought it wouldn't happen until we got where we're going... An odd mixture of relief and dread swirls inside me. Quickly, I run through my arguments again, but I've gone over them so often I've got them word perfect, despite my fear.

It's starting: the man behind the table speaks briefly in Arabic. Then the man who caught me steps forward and speaks in Arabic too. From his gestures and the few words I understand, he's describing my attempted escape. I wait for someone to translate, but when he's finished, the man behind the table begins to speak again. It sounds very formal.

I know one shouldn't speak without being spoken to in a court, but... it's hardly begun, yet everything in the judge's manner suggests *wrapping up*. A younger man by the door has just drawn a pistol from his belt: he inspects the magazine and snaps it home again. Then turns a hostile gaze on me. Hostile... and expectant.

"Please!" I gasp. "May I speak?"

"*You?*" says the judge scornfully, in accented English,

looking down at me at last. "Where are your witnesses?"

"My... my witnesses?"

"You are a woman, you must produce two witnesses for any statement you make, or your evidence is worthless. Where are your witnesses?"

It feels like ice is trickling down my spine. "I... I haven't got any..."

"Then how can you speak?" He lifts his gaze back to the men, dismissing me.

Witnesses. My stomach heaves and I barely manage to keep from vomiting all over the bare metal floor. How could I be so stupid? Me, Daniyah, future human rights lawyer... I know all about Sharia courts requiring women to produce witnesses. I've campaigned against it. Written blogs about it. I *know.*

So how could I have prepared arguments? Expected to have a voice here?

I know the answer. Of course. Because to allow myself to recognize that I would not be able to speak in my defence was to accept that there was no hope. No hope at all. Never was. I am a woman. I am nothing to them.

They will show no mercy.

I'm going to be a statistic: just one more corpse who wasn't 'Muslim' enough for them...

Tears are running down my cheeks, now; I can't stop them. The judge is speaking in Arabic again. Then the men are pulling me to my feet, leading me out into the passage. I whisper the *Shahada*, over and over. What else can I do?

Perhaps... nothing to lose... I yank with all my strength, twist free of one man... if I could get up to the deck... the other hits me so hard my head spins. I stumble along between them after that, barely able to stay on my feet as we go down the stairs. Sasha's sobs ring in my mind, mingling with my own... was it my fault? Did I miss the hair? Is this why this is happening to me...

RUTH

Something's afoot. The girls who were chosen as the new cooks brought lunch as usual, but now we've been told to get into our lines, as though for Arabic recitation. We wait uneasily, until...

Daniyah!

She's alive! Two of the men are half-dragging her through the door into the hold. A surge of joy makes me feel happier than I've been in days. Shannon, Daniyah's BFF, is practically bouncing up and down in her place, eyes shining. Where has Daniyah been? We all thought she was dead. What about the others? Are they alive as well?

The other men are filing in behind, lining up along the wall. Watching Daniyah. With... anticipation?

My joy begins to fade... What is going on?

DANIYAH

We're in the hold, now... Through my tears, I see the others, in their lines. I try to see Sasha, see how she is, but I'm shoved to my knees again. A black canvas bag is suddenly dragged over my head and everything is dark. A man is speaking formally in English. I catch 'traitor' and 'lesson to you all' but the fabric muffles sounds, and my heart is beating, faster and faster and faster, deafening me. My breathing is so loud. Loud and quick, far too quick...

"*La ilaha illa'llah...*" I whisper. *There is no God but God...* "*La ilaha illa'llah, Muhammadun rasul Allah...*"

Footsteps scuff behind me... a tiny click, like you hear in films...

"*La ilaha illa'llah,*" I sob. "*Muhammadun rasul Al...*"

RUTH

The shot is so loud my ears ring and I'm motionless in my place, just staring, staring... Daniyah's crumpled on the floor, her hand out-flung, and still, so totally still, just like Yoko.

The way she's lying looks so awkward... The thought drifts through my head but I know it's meaningless. Daniyah's dead. She can't feel it now.

"Good," says the leader briskly, and nods to the men who brought Daniyah in. They drag her body to the side, leaving a smear of blood across the deck. Shannon is crying hysterically, but the other men are watching the leader. They look eager. It wasn't just Daniyah's execution they were waiting for...

Daniyah's execution. I can't take my eyes off her limp hand, still visible in the corner. Feels like it should move, like she should just sit up and be okay... but she won't.

She's dead.

Am I going to die too?

A strange, cold feeling of terror seeps through me, permeating every part of me, echoing inside my head.

Poor Daniyah had no choice. But I do...

GEMMA

"On your feet!" the leader—Mr Evil, we call him, when we're sure no one can hear us—is ordering. An older, bearded stranger comes forward to stand beside him. "This is Sheikh Kabir: we are all honoured by his presence. His arrival means that this will be a happy day for some of you."

"These fine *Jihadis*," he waves to the men, "have requested that they be allowed to choose brides now. Since we still have many days of travel ahead of us, it has been decided to grant their request. Sheikh Kabir will act as your *wali*, and everyone will pay a bride price, so it will all be proper and above board. You do not need to speak; your silence will be deemed consent. The men will choose in order of seniority."

He gestures to the men, and one of the oldest comes forward and begins to walk up and down the lines, looking us over like we're cows he's thinking of buying. *Bride price*... he *is* buying one of us.

He stops in front of Jenny from year thirteen. "I have this one." He's one of the foreign men from the boat. Jenny goes white. The man takes her arm and tows her to the front. The men speak in Arabic; it sounds rather formal.

"Good," says the leader in English. "Now recite the *Shahada* for your new husband."

At the words 'new husband' Jenny sways slightly, like she's going to faint, and doesn't seem able to speak. Her 'husband' smacks her around the head and trembling, she manages to recite the necessary words in little more than a whisper.

"Good," says the leader again. "*Next.*"

Jenny is led away out of the hold, shaking. The next man is 'viewing' us. I feel physically sick and can't help counting the men. Sixteen more of them. I try to calculate my odds of being chosen, just as something to do to stop me from freaking out, but my mind won't work well enough.

My year seems popular. Because we're younger? I remember Mr Evil's remark about virgins, what seems a millennia ago outside school. If I'd managed to calculate the odds, I'd have to recalculate them now to take that into account...

After a while I manage to think of someone other than myself and glance at Annabel, quaking beside me, and Ruth on the other side, standing with a rather fixed expression in her eyes, like an animal at bay. Oh God-who-doesn't-exist, don't let them pick Ruth. How desirable does she look to those men? She's not skinny as a rake, couldn't be called fat either—but that's exactly the sort of girl they're picking. She's only pretty, though, not drop dead beautiful.

Oh no, poor Kris... she's just been picked by the man who raped her. She sobs her way through the *Shahada* and the man drags her off.

Ten men left.

Six men left.

Are we going to make it?

Three men left...

But this man's slowing down, looking us over much more carefully. No, looking Ruth over... I don't want to draw his attention to me, I don't, but... how seriously is he considering Ruth?

He puts out a hand and jerks her chin up, inspecting her face. I can see her fists clench, see her start to tremble. He opens his mouth...

I don't really decide to do it, I just find myself... doing it... "What about me, sir? I'd make you a good wife. Better than her, sir. She's a useless cook..."

RUTH

My heart clenches in shock and gratitude at what Gemma's trying to do... but the man smacks Gemma across the face with the back of his hand, sending her staggering against Annabel. "You think I am not able to choose a woman, insolent girl!"

"She really is a very bad cook..." The thin, terrified voice is Annabel's. Love for both my friends pushes the terror aside, just slightly... "You're such a strong, brave *Jihadi*, you should have a good wife..."

She flinches as the man raises his hand to hit her as well. "No, don't spoil her face," says the man behind him. I remember him from the school. "I want the long hair girl. Unless you want her?"

"No. I have chosen *this one*," he grabs my shoulder and pulls me forward. "She has good hips and is pleasing to the eye. She will learn to cook, or feel my displeasure."

He drags me the short distance to the Sheikh and I fight desperately to stay calm, to *think*... There's no point objecting to the marriage—it wouldn't hold a drop of water in a court of law, anyway—but the *words*... I can't say those words... Could I try to mumble something and hope they don't make me say it clearly? But that's not the point, really...

Annabel has been dragged forward as well and the formal Arabic is already being spoken and then... I'm married—according to them, anyway.

"The *Shahada*," orders the leader.

My mind is close to melting in panic. Yoko is flashing before my eyes, bleeding, dying, I can see Daniyah's lifeless body without even turning my head, I'm fighting not to vomit...

I feign a coughing fit. No real point in stalling, but I can't *think*...

"Fine, you first," the leader turns to Annabel.

Annabel goes dead white, catches my eye, then looks away. Catches it again.

"Say it!" yells Gemma.

"Shut it!" the leader yells back.

Annabel's husband scowls and unsheathes a knife from his belt. Grabs her by the hair and touches it to her throat. "I've paid good money for you!" he snaps, "but I'll see you dead before I have an infidel wife! Say the *Shahada*."

Annabel squeezes her eyes shut, beginning to cry. And between the sobs, she says it. The man relaxes and sheathes the knife. "Good," he says, patting her bum as one would pat a dog "Good girl. Perhaps you'll do after all."

"Now you," says the leader, pointing fiercely at me, as though Annabel's resistance has made him suspicious of my coughing. "*Say it.*"

This is it. I have to decide now. I've already decided, of course. It's not changing my mind that's the problem.

"I will not," I whisper.

Pain explodes through my scalp as my 'husband' grabs my hair and yanks my head back. I feel the knife against my throat, the line of fire as the edge nicks my skin.

"You are my wife! You will say it!"

Something is running down my face... tears. I'm crying. But an image comes into my mind, a man on a cross, an innocent man, in agony... for me. And words, familiar words...

He will keep you firm to the end...

I may not have the strength to hold firm, but He does.

"I will not." My voice is slightly stronger this time. I close my eyes. Reach for God. Wait.

"SAY IT! *Say the creed, NOW!*" He shakes me, making the knife cut deeper into my neck and it hurts, it hurts...

Lord, be with me, be with me, be with me... I struggle to keep my eyes shut. Better words are on the tip of my tongue and I murmur them, "I believe in God; the Father, Son and Holy Spirit..."

He hears me. I'm flung to the floor, so hard it hurts, and he's kicking me, and that hurts too, and I curl into a ball to try and protect myself but his feet are everywhere, and I just want it to stop, but I mustn't, mustn't, mustn't say it...

Lord, be with me, be with me, be with me...

He's stopped. The pain eases. Only now do I hear Gemma screaming, "Say it!" like she's been screaming it for a while. And Annabel, sobbing, "Say it, Ruth, please!"

I lie, shaking in terror and sobbing in pain, and refuse to open my eyes. The few men that are left are laughing at my 'husband'.

"You've wasted your money on that one!" sniggers one. "Should have listened to the insolent girl, shouldn't you?"

Apparently this remark is hilarious.

Rough hands grab me, drag me up into a kneeling position. The knife digs against my throat. *Ow...*

"SAY IT NOW!"

Oh Lord, this is it, isn't it? Oh, be with me, be with me, be with me...

My lips want to open, almost of their own accord, and save the physical body they're part of.

Be with me... But He is. I feel the warmth of His love. And I keep my lips shut.

The pain in my neck is suddenly agony and there's blood, and I can't breathe, and I'm choking, choking just like Yoko, and all I can think is *there's no way you bastards can make me say it now, so ya boo, sucks to you* and *Lord, You're with me, You're with me, You're with me, You're with me, You're...*

GEMMA

Annabel's screaming and sobbing, half the girls in the room are sobbing, and I'm just standing, staring at Ruth, lying there on the floor in a pool of blood, eyes blank, just like Yoko—she had a funny smile on her face but now it's gone slack and empty, so empty. I can't believe she did it, can't believe they did it, just can't believe... *it*.

Not Ruth. Not *Ruth*. Anyone but Ruth.

How can someone so good die like that?

This is like, the ultimate proof there's no God. No anything.

Ruth wouldn't agree, but then she's not here to see it.

The man wipes his knife on a clean bit of Ruth's robe and sheathes it. Strides towards me. Before I know what he's doing he's grabbed a handful of my robe and hauled me to the front. Cold sweat breaks out all over me—my tears trail off abruptly, frozen by terror—*is he going to kill me because I was shouting so loud?*

"I will take this one instead!" He slaps me around the head. "And she will be as good a wife as she claims." He slaps me again. "Or she will join my first wife in hell!" Yet another whack.

The leader smirks, as though all this is terribly amusing, but speaks the formal Arabic, and moments later I seem to be married.

"Say it," orders my husband.

I recite quickly and clearly. In a respectful voice. With my eyes demurely cast down. I don't know how I do it. I'm shaking with rage as well as with grief.

But I know now what I have to do. I have to survive. And someday, when my husband is asleep, and there's a chance I'll get away, I'll take his knife, or a brick, or anything heavy or sharp enough, and I'll go all Judith on him. Ruth used to tell me about Judith whenever I complained there were no strong women in the Bible. That's what I'll do. I'll end his evil existence. I'll kill him for Ruth, for what he did to her. For what he's going to do to me. For Yoko and Daniyah.

And I'll escape.

And I'll live.

Someday. He thinks I'm nothing. He won't watch his back. He'll learn.

Ruth wouldn't like it.

But she just lost her vote.

ANNABEL

Gemma bows her head meekly and follows the man who just murdered Ruth. To me she looks about as meek as a basking adder, but the man looks pleased and struts out of the hold. Thinks he's got a good one this time. I suspect he's going to get a nasty surprise sooner or later. Gemma looked ready to do murder when he... when he killed...

Ruth's still there on the floor. Ruth's body. I force myself to look at it again, 'cause it's probably the last time I'll see her. Until I get to heaven too. If I do, after what I just did.

I feel the shame, eating into me like acid. But if I ever had any doubts about God, they're gone. Ruth's erased them with her courage, with that little smile that told me more clearly than any words that God was with her in those last dreadful moments.

She was crying. She was so afraid. But she held firm. Because God was with her.

And I know what I want. Of myself. And I think it's what the Lord wants of me too. And I'm going to pray and pray and pray, until I can do it. I want to be strong enough—or have enough of the Lord's strength—to just stand up and say, 'I'm a Christian. I don't care what you think, I'm Christian.' Come what will.

It's not going to happen today.

Or tomorrow.

Or the next day.

But someday.

It's what I'm going to do.

LOUISE

There's no more water. It ran out... I can't quite seem to remember when. Today we couldn't even sit by the door and look out. Couldn't drag ourselves up from the floor. My head aches. My body aches. My lips are bleeding.

I say the Lord's Prayer in my head, over and over. Over and over. It's the only prayer I know. The sun's dropping. It's cooling down. Soon we'll be too cold, instead of too hot. I ought to find my hood, put it around me, but I can't make myself move. I just lie, and the prayer goes around and around my head. But God doesn't seem to hear.

I suppose we'll die soon...

RISHAD

The prayer vigil is over, but the beach is still packed. Loads of people who've travelled a long way are enjoying a bit of time to unwind by the sea before going home. Just like me and Isaar. This isn't the exact spot where the body washed ashore, but it's close. They clearly chose it because there's a large car park with public toilets, and a food van. All of which are swamped by the numbers but are better than nothing.

"There was a really good turnout," says Isaar. We've got along the beach a bit, away from the crowds, and he's been crouched motionless by a rock pool for several minutes. From the way his eyes are now tracking here and there, his patience has paid off.

"Yeah. Anything good in there?"

"There are some quite pretty little fish. And something's hiding in the seaweed in the corner; I'm not quite sure what it is. You know, I'm more than ready for something to eat."

"What, pretty little fish?"

"I'd rather not."

"Well, I can see the queue at the food van from here and it doesn't look good."

"Oh." Isaar looks over his shoulder, up towards the top of the beach. "See what you mean." He leaves his rock pool and comes to sit by me again. "I suppose we could head home; get something on route. Seems a bit of a shame to go so soon, that's all."

Before I can reply, our phones buzz in our pockets.

"I wonder if Sam *is* here," I say, pulling mine out and checking the message. Yes, Sam.

> Finally spotted u down there
> on the rocks (I think!). Near
> the front of the food q, do u
> want anything?

"Brilliant," I say, and text him back.

> Yes please. We'll eat
> (almost) anything!

ISAAR

Sam comes over balancing three cardboard fast food cartons and an armful of bottled drinks and climbs up to us. "Here you go," he says, handing one of each to both of us. "Beef burger and chips, and juice. Hasn't been near a pig, I checked."

"Great, thanks, Sam," I say.

"Yeah, Isaar was about to tuck into the contents of that rock pool!" says Rish.

"What, is there actually something in there?" says Sam. "I never see anything in those things."

"You have to be patient," I say. I don't offer to pay him for the food, and nor does Rish. We can both tell it's an apology.

Rish murmurs the *Basmala* and bites into his burger with unfeigned appreciation. "I am so ready for this."

"I thought the vigil went well," says Sam, opening his own food box. "It was great those imams got up to do prayers—and people of other religions, too."

"Wouldn't have been much of a multi-faith vigil otherwise," points out Rish.

"S'pose not," concedes Sam. "What did I interrupt, anyway?"

"Oh, we were just talking about odds," says Rish. "Like, what are the odds that crazy girl playing the violin on that next lot of rocks is the shy violinist we saw take out that bastard in

Oxford on Friday."

"Bastard? Not the guy who got arrested from your mosque?"

It's been in the papers already.

"Yeah, him," says Rish grimly, then brightens, "Anyway, this dodgy convert gives the police the slip, and comes sprinting out of the mosque. And Isaar and I are getting ready to do our manly best to try and stop him—and paying no attention to this pretty white girl playing the violin a little way down the road, I admit. Nor is the guy, because he runs right past her, and get this, she chucks her music stand straight out in front of him! Wham. He went down like a felled tree. It was hilarious." He sobers. "Or would have been, if it wasn't for the larger situation."

"And she's over there, *right now?*"

"Well, Isaar's convinced it's her. I'm not sure I looked hard enough at her on Friday to be certain. I think the odds are too long. We're in *Norfolk*, it's a long way from Oxford."

"But *we're* from Oxford," points out Sam. "At least in term time. And if you want to talk about odds, well, what are the odds that there's another pair of Asian identical twins on this beach? From Oxford."

"No way," says Rish.

"Not really?" I say.

"Really. I saw them during the vigil. Two little boys; here with their mum and a group from the Oxford Catholic churches, from the banner they have with them. The kids had their hands together, praying ever so hard—cute but kind of embarrassing."

"Embarrassing?" queries Rish.

"Yeah, they were fidgeting less than I was!"

We snort at that. Easy enough to imagine Sam dutifully standing through all those prayers, bored out of his mind. He doesn't exactly have what one would call an active prayer life.

"And they were actually identical?" I check.

"Peas in a pod, Isaar."

"Well," I shrug. "*Insha'Allah.*"

106

A fleeting tightness crosses Sam's face, then he smiles and takes another bite of his burger. "So, future doctor," he teases, "what do you think of our nutrition tonight?"

TERESA

I'm playing to God, because the surf drowns out the music, but that's all right. I came along here so no one would think I was trying to collect money or anything. I stood through all the spoken prayers of the vigil, tried my best to pray them the way Mum would have done, but it was hard to concentrate for so long. Now it's over, I'm happy to stand on these high rocks, out of reach of the splashes from the wild sea, and play.

Bit stupid to bring my violin to something like this, my irreplaceable violin—Mum's violin—but right now, I'm glad I did.

LOUISE

I must've been dozing. When I drag my eyes open, there's an older girl sitting on the edge of the life raft, in the doorway, brown hair falling around her face. She smiles at me when I look at her. I know her; she's a year eleven, always busy at the CU, though she holds no official position. Younger girls often take their problems to her. And older girls...

"Ruth, how did you escape?" I gasp.

Her mouth quirks slightly. "The hard way." She shrugs as though it's not important. "We'd better see about getting to land, don't you think?"

"We don't have a sail," I tell her despairingly. "Or even a paddle."

"That's okay," she smiles. "I brought one." She holds up a short wooden paddle, then dips it into the water.

We begin to move, I can see the clouds spinning and reforming above, moving far faster than seems credible. I watch them for a long time, still praying the prayer. "Aren't you getting tired," I ask eventually.

"I'm fine. Relax. We're near the shore. But keep praying. This is the tricky bit."

JOHN

"Well, we can still see the *lights*," I say.

We both know when Mama said we could play on the beach, but 'don't go out of sight', she didn't *mean* the lights, but... the next outcrop of rocks looks even more interesting than the last three. Or four. Or is it five, now? We've come too far, and it's not like us to disobey Mama, but...

"Just this one more," James says. "Since we're almost there. Then we'll go straight back."

"Straight back," I agree.

We break into a jog across the sand, then scramble quickly to the top of the rocks. This whole kidnapped girls thing really ruined our seventh birthday, but today we got a trip to the beach, and it counts as praying for the girls! Well, we *did* pray for the girls, for hours, until Mama said we'd done our bit and we could go and play.

"It's like a rock castle!" James says, circling the top of the outcrop.

"Yeah..." I'm looking down at where the waves are crashing on the rocks. The sea's rough today. When I look up at the horizon, I notice how dark it's getting. "James, there's either going to be a storm, or it's really late! We've got to get back! Mama will be worried!"

James frowns at the sky as well. "Yeah... we'd better go."

I turn to climb back down the rocks, but something catches my eye. I look out along the next beach... there, in the water. "What's that?"

James hops back up to join me. "What?"

"There? Something orange, see..."

"It looks like a..."

We look at each other. "A life raft?" we both say. We saw a film recently, with a life raft...

"Do you think there's someone in it?" I say.

"I suppose there must be. Why would it be floating around empty?"

We're both scrambling down the other side of the rocks, now. We reach the beach and stare at the orange object going up and down on the sea, out beyond the breaking waves. It's definitely a blow-up life raft thing. "Should we try and get it?"

James grabs my arm as I move towards the water. "It's too far out! We're too small! We need grown-ups!"

A wave rolls in, taller than we are, and breaks on the sand. He's right. "Okay... well, I'm the faster runner, I'll get help! You stay here and make sure it doesn't go out of sight."

James nods. "*Run!*" he urges.

JAMES

John takes off back down the beach, goes up the rocks like a monkey and disappears from sight. I move along the beach to keep the raft in sight, and looking back, soon I see him going over the next outcrop. The raft's getting away already. I follow it again, and that's when it sinks in.

All along this long beach, these spines of rocks run into the sea, breaking up the sand. And the raft's being carried straight towards the next lot. *Oh no...*

"Lord, what do I do?" I whisper. I run to catch up with the raft again. "Hello?" I shout at the top of my voice. "Hello in the raft... hello? You need to swim to the beach! Hello? Can you hear me?"

No reply. No movement. It's still heading for the rocks. I imagine how long it will take John to reach the main beach, for people to come back...

They'll be too late, won't they?

JOHN

I scramble to the top of the third outcrop, panting, pleased with the speed I'm going. Taking a quick rest, I look back, trying to see James. There...

Wait, he's... *Oh Lord! He's going into the sea! No! What's he doing?*

Actually, why's he so much further along the beach? Then I look at the rocks, and I understand. The raft's being driven onto them.

And James is trying to stop it.

A lump of fear choking me, I leap down the other side of the outcrop and sprint flat out towards those glowing lights.

"Help!" I yell. *"Help!"*

JAMES

I run straight into the sea and dive into the first wave as it looms over me—surface, spluttering and gasping at the cold. I start wading forward, but the next wave's coming already. I dive into that and wade again. The waves knock me back each time, but finally I'm beyond the breakers. And out of my depth. I start swimming, looking frantically for the raft.

There... it's swooping up and down on the waves, visible and then hidden again, but finally, after an age of being tossed and bumped about by the waves, I reach it and grab onto the cord that's around the edge. I hang on, half-crying in fear. The power of the sea makes me feel totally helpless—I'm cold and exhausted already.

When I've recovered slightly, I pull myself around the raft and look in at the door. Two older girls are lying inside, dressed in baggy black robes. "Hello?" I shout. *"Hello?"* Can they jump out and swim to shore? Would that be easier?

But they don't even stir. So I get a good hold on that cord with one hand and start swimming towards the beach. I swim hard for what feels like several minutes, but when I look around, the rocks are closer. A lot closer.

I'm not achieving *anything!* What shall I do? I could swim back to the beach myself, *maybe...* but the girls seem so ill. If the raft goes on the rocks they'll drown.

Lord, send me some big strong men, I pray silently. *Please send*

110

them right now! Please?

TERESA

The tide's coming up. Or perhaps the sea's just getting rougher. It's gone unnaturally dark. There must be a storm coming. Either way, the salt splashes are getting closer. Although the metal bench set into the top of these rocks suggests that the sea rarely covers them completely, I crouch down and put my violin into its case. I can't have so long before I need to get the bus to the town to catch my train.

"Help!" I hear a faint cry and look up. A little Asian boy is running along the beach as though every monster from every closet in the world is chasing him. "Help!" he screams.

I jump down off the rocks and hurry to him. "Hey, what's wrong?"

"Life raft," he sobs, almost too out of breath to talk at all. "In... the water! Going onto... rocks... My twin... gone in... after it! Help him, please!"

"Did you say *twin?*" I ask, shooting a horrified look at the boisterous sea. There's a kid in there? *His* age? "*Where is he?*"

The boy points back along the beach. "Five lots of rocks," he gasps.

That far? "Get more people!" I tell him. "I'll go and help him!"

With one anguished thought for my violin, lying up there on the rocks, I turn and sprint off along the beach.

SAM

"I still think we should go and say hi," Isaar is saying.

"She was wearing a cross, you know," says Rish. "And she looked pretty young. She's probably still at school."

"I said say *hi*, not ask her on a date!"

"I thought you were allowed to marry Christians," I can't help saying.

"Yeah, *allowed* to," says Rish. "But our faith's too important

111

to us for us to deliberately date someone who doesn't share it."

"Fair enough." I wouldn't win any prizes for regular church attendance, but I feel a bit the same way. Then I put my food box down suddenly and rise to my feet. "Heads up, I think something's wrong..."

I've just seen a little boy tearing along the beach in a way that doesn't look like running for fun. In fact, it's one of the twins who were standing near me at the vigil. Isaar's pretty violinist has just hurried to speak to him. After only a few words, she turns and races off the way the boy came from—the kid runs on.

I scramble down the rocks quickly to intercept him. "What's up?"

"Life raft in the water. My twin went in after it!" he gasps. "Five lots of rocks... that way," he points.

Twin? Merciful God, no wonder that girl was running so fast!

Rish and Isaar are already pounding away across the sand.

"Hey kid, look up there," I say quickly, "you see that wooden hut, with the red and yellow sign? That's the life guard. You run straight up there and tell them, understand? *Go!*"

JAMES

However hard I try to swim, it's not doing any good at all. The rocks are coming closer and closer. And I don't know what to do. If I stop trying, the raft will be lost, and the girls with it. Except trying isn't working. But I feel so cold and weak now, I'm afraid to let go and try to reach the shore by myself.

Lord, help me! I kick out frantically, uselessly. *Lord, help us!*

I catch a glimpse of movement on the beach. A figure, racing into the water. *Yes! We're saved. Thank you, Lord!*

As the figure gets beyond the breakers and half-swims, half-wades towards us, I see that it's a young woman. Only a couple of years older than the girls in the raft. But she reaches us and grabs hold of the cord.

"Are you all right?" she asks.

I nod, my teeth chattering. "I can't get it away from the rocks," I sniff.

She starts heaving on the raft, but every time a wave rolls in it lifts her off her feet. The rocks aren't getting any nearer now, but we're getting no closer to the beach, either... Her best efforts are only enough to keep us in the same place.

Lord, I don't mean to be ungrateful, but this is why I asked You for big strong men, you know...

The girl keeps hauling that raft towards the beach every time her feet touch the bottom—she eyes the shore and mutters, "Come on, come on, *someone...*" She must be getting tired. I try to kick a bit harder, to help her, but my legs feel like jellyfish tentacles.

There! Three larger figures are ploughing into the sea in a cloud of spray, striding out towards us. Three young men. Phew, God got it right this time. They catch hold of the raft and begin to tow it to shore, keeping their footing as the waves roll past.

"Up you go, kid," says the white guy, tipping me onto the raft, on top of the roof covering. I flop along the inflatable rim and hold on, too tired to be anything but grateful.

They hold the raft tightly as we reach the breakers, fighting to keep it under control, but more people are rushing into the sea now to help, and the many hands keep the raft right way up despite the sea's best efforts. It's hauled quickly up the sand.

I lie there and shiver, until the guy who put me on the raft sits me up and wraps a jacket around me. Dry, so he must've thrown it off before running into the sea. "Hey, you're not injured?"

I shake my head, teeth chattering like mad. "Jus' cold."

"Well, I expect an ambulance is on the way by now. They'll check you over."

"I'm fine," I protest.

He looks amused. "Well, just sit there and keep that jacket around you, and you should warm up a bit."

TERESA

Thank God for young men. How easily they got that raft to shore. Admittedly there were three of them, and then many more, but still, what a relief. I'm actually not sure which three they were, now all these extra people are here. One was white and I think two were Asian but that's all I remember.

I feel cold and wobbly from the exertion, but the other people, mostly men, are hanging back, so I climb into the raft quickly and try to rouse the girls. "Hello? Can you hear me? You're safe now..."

Someone by the entrance pushes a pair of jackets into my hands; I tuck them over the girls. The smaller one, a mousy looking girl who appears to be no more than fourteen, is stirring slightly.

"Can you hear me?" I ask.

"Yes," she murmurs. Her lips are cracked and bleeding.

"Has anyone got any water?" asks the person who's hovering outside the entrance—a young Asian man. "They're showing clear symptoms of dehydration..."

"Are you from Chisbrook?" I ask the girl who's conscious.

"That's our school..." she whispers. "They took us..."

"They're from Chisbrook!" I call over my shoulder. The babble of noise grows exponentially.

The girl is trying to lift her head and look around.

"Take it easy," I tell her. "An ambulance will be along soon."

"Ruth..." she's saying. "Where's Ruth?"

"There, she's right there beside you, it's okay."

"No, that's Kim. Where's *Ruth*?"

I look around the tiny interior of the life raft, my heart sinking. "Are you saying there was another girl with you?"

"She was right here... She was paddling..."

There's no other girl, and no paddle. Heavy-hearted, I stand up quickly. "There was a third girl!" I shout. "She must've gone overboard!"

With a dismayed moan, the growing crowd lurches towards

114

the sea, but a young man raises his voice firmly, "Stay out of the water, everyone! This is a job for the coastguard! If any of us go out there, they'll just have to rescue *us* first! Climb up on the rocks and look from there, and search the beach."

Is he one of the guys who pulled the raft ashore? When he heads off towards the rocks, and an Asian guy follows him, I suspect so, but it's too late to thank them now. They're busy looking out over the sea and checking along the rocks in case the missing girl has been washed onto them. Other people join them, scatter along the next bit of beach, searching.

The Asian guy in the doorway is passing me a bottle of water he's got from someone. "Here, just give her small sips. She mustn't have too much at once."

He sounds like he knows what he's talking about, so I crouch beside the girl again. "Here's water. Just a sip, though..." I add quickly, as her thin fingers close around the bottle like a baby bird's claws. Then she glimpses the knowledgeable guy and flinches back, terror spilling into her eyes.

He ducks back out of sight. His voice comes, a little strained: "Ah, here's the life guard. I'll go and help look for the other girl, then."

I hear him move away, but I'm so busy concentrating on getting the frightened girl to drink again that it's only after he's gone that it occurs to me he was probably the third guy who pulled us out of the sea.

JAMES

The girls are from Chisbrook! How wonderful! I was so afraid they were going to drown! Me too.

Where's John? And Mama, she must be crazy with worry by now. I'd better go and find them. In a minute. My legs still feel like water. I hug the jacket closer as another bout of shivering shakes me.

The sound of an engine makes me look up. A red quad bike is roaring along the beach. The lifeguard. John is clinging behind him, and loads more people are jogging after them, looks of curiosity on their faces.

"James!" yells John, jumping down as soon as the bike stops. "Are you okay?"

"I'm fine..." The lifeguard is humping a big first aid bag over to the life raft, and disappearing inside. I get my feet under me at last, and stand up. "Let's find Mama."

Quickly, before the ambulance comes... because they'll *fuss*, oh, will they *fuss*, and they might even want to stick needles in me or something...

But we've barely gone three steps when Mama is rushing towards us. "Boys! Where have you *been?*" She gathers us to her, and looks at me in shock. "James, you're all wet, what have you been *doing?* Whose coat is that?"

"A guy put it round me. I helped pull the raft to shore, Mama, that's all."

"You went *into the sea?* What were you thinking? There are loads of grown-ups here to do that!"

"I know, sorry Mama." I wonder what it will say in the newspaper tomorrow, and whether I'll be busted. Oh well.

"What are you *doing* along here, anyway?" she demands slipping her jacket off and wrapping it around me as well. "I said to *stay in sight!* I've been looking for you for hours!"

"Sorry, Mama," says John contritely. "We went too far."

"*Too far?*" But she glances up at an approaching group of reporters and gets to her feet, taking our hands. "Come on, let's get back. Everyone is waiting. You'd better leave that coat here, James, there are some dry clothes in the minibus that I brought in case one of you fell in a rock pool. Come on..."

Reluctantly, I let the jacket fall from beneath hers and she leads us quickly away, letting go of John in order to raise a hand to hide her face from the looming cameras.

TERESA

The flashing lights of the ambulance, parked up on the road, bounce across the beach. The girls are surrounded by paramedics and I'm totally superfluous now. The third girl's

116

nowhere to be found along the shore, and people are beginning to leave.

I glance at my watch. Yikes! The last bus that will get me to the train station on time is leaving in minutes! The fifty pounds was enough for a cheap advance fare, but it's non-transferable and I can't afford a new ticket.

There's nothing more I can do here, anyway. As if to confirm this, a search and rescue helicopter clatters overhead. Even the hunt for the third girl is being taken over by those better placed for success. I should catch my bus.

I turn and jog as quickly as I can along the beach, climbing over all the rocks. My heart is in my mouth as I scramble up the last outcrop, up to the metal bench. The case is still there. I crouch, open it, just to check. My violin nestles inside, undamaged. My Mum's violin. I close the clasps securely and hug the case for a moment.

It's nothing compared to three lives, but I'm still glad to have it back safe and sound.

I check my watch again, put the case on my back, and run.

SAM

"I am absolutely flipping freezing," says Rish, as we're finally heading back along the beach. "Uh-oh, watch out..."

I switch off the light on my phone quickly, and we all crouch behind a nearby boulder, waiting for the roaming reporter to go past. My clothes are still damp—even my jacket's damp after the kid had it round him. I rub my hands together, shivering. Thunder has been rumbling for a while, and big drops of rain are just starting to plop down. Soon we'll be as wet as we were when we came out of the sea. I'm better off than Rish and Isaar, though—their jackets got whisked off to hospital with the girls.

"I can't stand it when someone does the right thing and then it's all over the paper like they did something extra-ordinary," Isaar mutters, as we wait.

I can picture the headlines all too easily. "Hero Students in

117

Life Raft Rescue?" I suggest.

"What we did was *normal*, not *heroic*," snorts Rish. "Or it blinking well ought to be!"

"That little boy should be on the front page, not us," I say softly. "Okay, it was *really* inadvisable, but it was still incredibly brave. And your pretty violinist is a plucky girl, Isaar. Ran straight in without hesitating, though she's not that big."

"She's not *my* anything," protests Isaar. "Okay, I think he's gone..."

Soon we're glumly surveying the mess the wind—and the seagulls—have left of our interrupted meal. It's after midnight now, and the search has been called off. Apparently the doctors and investigators managed to question the girls a bit more, and learned that only the two of them escaped from the ship, and that they didn't see the third girl in the raft until they'd been drifting without food and with barely any water for almost a week. When the forensics team confirmed that only two girls had been in the life raft, they concluded that the other girl was only a hallucination.

I don't know whether to be relieved or not. One less girl free, but... not a girl fallen overboard and drowned, either.

"This is a dead loss," says Rish, picking up the wind-strewn food boxes. "Let's for pity's sake get up to the car, find a twenty-four-hour services and get some hot coffee."

"*Insha'Allah,*" says Isaar, with feeling.

"I second that proposal," I say.

JASPER

The smells of New Wellington boots, dog and strong mints waft to my nose as I thread the leather thong through the last rabbit's hock.

"Hi, William," I say, without looking around.

"You're uncanny, boy, you know that?" booms a friendly voice from a few meters along the hedge.

"No, I just pay attention to the world around me," I say dryly. "It's my dad who's the uncanny one, according to you, anyway."

"Now, I'm glad to see you all," says the farmer, letting himself into the field, "but Margery and I, we mean it about the dabbling. He's to do none of it on our land. It may or may not bring him good fortune, but it leaves troubles behind it, no doubt about it."

"He knows. And he does stick to it, you know." I hang my bunch of rabbits on a jutting out bit of hedge and crouch beside the nearest hole, removing the net. "Now, let's see if I can get my little beauty back..."

Making my calling noise, I waft a raisin in the mouth of the hole and place it a few feet away, then go back to William, plucking a clover flower and sucking on the flower stems, then munching it up. Yum. Glance around to catch him looking at me in a rather worried way.

"What?"

"Clever lad like you, you should be in school."

"School!" I go cold at the thought. "*Hecate, queen of night,* no! Two terms was enough!"

Dad, in a fit of reversion to his middle class bricks and mortar upbringing, suddenly decided to send me to school a few years ago, when I was twelve. It's been my image of Hades ever since. There were no plants, no animals, horrible artificial food, and the other children spoke some foreign language all about Single Directions and X Factoids and a million incomprehensible things.

Wasn't long before I told Dad he could either take me out of school again or I'd take myself off entirely. He knew I'd neither starve—nor be found unless I wanted to be—so no more school it was.

"Seriously, William, what would I want to go back to school for?" I shudder.

"Don't you want friends your own age? GCSEs?"

"I'm doing *some* GCSEs. I read loads of books. And I'm happy with the friends I've got." I nod towards the as-yet-uneaten raisin and to the piebald pony grazing nearby. "Why're you nagging me all of a sudden?"

119

William sighs a bit apologetically. "Oh, I suppose with what happened last month..."

Last month... A coldness runs through me, as though a cloud has just covered the sun. "Those girls that were kidnapped? They've got them back by now, right?"

I haven't been listening to the news. Or reading the newspapers, for that matter. Whenever I do, there seems to be a hundred things that remind me of... that day.

"No, they haven't, nor look likely to." He sighs even more heavily. "They'll never have a chance to take their exams now. Look what was released this morning... s'why I felt like a walk, to be honest..." He pulls out a shiny new smart phone and begins prodding it with a large finger.

"Seriously, William?" I tease, to hide the fact that my stomach is trembling as though full of frightened butterflies. I don't want to think about this. I can see it again, in my head, those girls lying there...

He flushes slightly. "My son bought it for me. It's actually quite useful... in a slightly frustrating way... ah-ha, there it is..." He hands it to me and I accept it reluctantly. But I never told anyone what happened, so I have to pretend nothing's wrong.

I peer at the small screen. We don't even have a telly in the caravan—and I'm certainly quite happy to keep it that way. Normally it would make a change to see a video, though.

But not this one... A man with eyes like a rabid animal is ranting about how *Allah* told him to take those girls as slaves, and how he is going to sell them... how girls shouldn't be in school... all girls over nine should be married...

"What is that guy *on*?"

William just sighs yet again.

There are the girls... all dressed in grey and black, staring out of the screen, sad and solemn. Reciting something. Some of them hardly look much older than me. Just like the girls in the horsebox.

"I tell you," I say, as the video finishes, and anger is coiling in my stomach, driving the butterflies into an even greater frenzy, "if I met that man I'd put him down like a mad dog!

Why doesn't someone do something?"

"You don't keep up with the news enough, Jasper my boy. Government's had two bombs and a machete attack to deal with just since those girls were taken. Things are getting worse."

He sounds so grave it sends a shiver down my spine. And a shard of guilt. I live in my happy little world of fields and woods, but others aren't so lucky. "Perhaps... I will try and listen to the news a bit more often." My heart sinks at the thought.

"I reckon you should. Ah, there's your ferret..."

I'm already handing the phone back—I bend and scoop the warm furry form into my arms, hugging her for a moment. That video is terrible... no, not the video, what's happened. Those poor girls, I just assumed they'd be found...

William seems so worried.

Perhaps I really had better pay a bit more attention to the news.

If I can bear it...

ALLELUIA

Cathie was being interviewed on the news with me today, for the three-month anniversary. They tried to get her to speak about the kidnapping a few times, but all she wanted to talk about was how things were going at college. The British universities were falling over themselves to give us places, despite the fact we never finished our exams. I got interviewed alongside three Deans of Admissions on one occasion and they were practically fighting over me on live television.

"I try not to think about what happened," Cathie kept telling them. I understand how she feels, of course, but I can't stop watching that video, over and over. Everyone who was shown on screen was okay a couple of months ago—at least physically—but there's no way to know about Ruth and the others who're presumably refusing to convert. Or if they are. Becky wasn't there so she probably really is dead, as Louise and Kim feared. They might *all* be...

No. The others are *okay*. They are. And I *will not* stop talking about what happened until they're all safe. People are forgetting already. I'm just some sort of celebrity, now. They ask me about college—uni, they call it here—they ask me about my parents' work, do I have a boyfriend... But I slip it in, here and there, as the Lord moves me, reminding them what happened, what's *still* happening to the others.

What would I give to stop, to become anonymous again... but I've gotta make sure the cameras keep coming. Gotta be funny, and interesting, and tear up in public, though I'd much rather shut myself in my room when I need to have a good cry, which is too often, nowadays.

Because if people get bored with me, I can't help my friends anymore.

But how long will I have to keep this up?

Lord, work through me...

JOHN

Mama's watching the morning news, but I'm far more interested in the fork fight I'm having with James. Any moment now Mama will tell us to stop it, but I'm winning... I pin James's fork down on the plate, twisting my own fork so he can't yank it free. "Surrender?"

"You wish!" my twin giggles.

I can see him preparing for some tricksy fork-freeing manoeuvre. I prepare to resist, giggling too. Then I realize James isn't paying attention anymore, he's looking at Mama. What's wrong?

Mama's holding her glass of breakfast juice so tightly her knuckles look like a white person's. And staring at the screen.

A man in a TV studio is speaking, very grave-faced, and some words are scrolling across the bottom:

BREAKING NEWS: 4 CHISBROOK SCHOOLGIRLS WALK TO FREEDOM

"Have more of them escaped?" I ask James.

"Looks like it."

"Shhh, you two," murmurs Mama, pushing back a few strands of ebony hair. We think she's the most beautiful woman in the world, and we're proud to have lovely brown skin like hers, even if the bullies at school call us names sometimes. But she's trying to listen, her dark eyes intent on the screen, so we listen too.

"On a less cheerful note, the escapees have reported the deaths of at least eight other girls, four of whom were killed on the journey from England almost six months ago. One of these four, Ruth Kerril, a girl of just sixteen, was beaten viciously before having her throat cut after she refused to convert to Islam. Christians of all denominations are already calling her death a martyrdom."

I shudder, that video creeping back into my mind. But then I remember something. "Wasn't Ruth the third girl in the raft?" I whisper to James.

"Yeah," he says. Thoughtfully. He's gone a bit pale, and I know he's thinking of the video too.

"We are joined now in the studio by Alleluia Williams." The camera backs up a bit to show a familiar near-black face, just now tight and closed and unusually not-smiley. I feel James sit up slightly beside me. Alleluia may not be Catholic, but oh my, does she have a passion for the Lord!

"Alleluia, thank you for joining us at such short notice. And especially after receiving such tragic news... just last night, is that correct?"

Alleluia nods. "Yes, I got a call..." She stops and clears her throat before going on. "I got a call just when I was going to bed. They said Shannon and the others had escaped and they were okay and I was so happy. But..." her voice shakes... "then they told me about Ruth and Becky and Daniyah and the others..."

"And can I ask how you felt when you heard the news about Ruth? You used to run the Christian Union together, I believe?"

Alleluia nods and rubs a hand across her cheek, brushing a tear away. "Well, I cried. I cried so hard. All this time I've been hoping and praying she was alive, but she... Well, I just cried and cried. But... But all the while I kept saying *thank God, thank you, God, praise you, God!* Because she held firm! She didn't deny Him! 'Cos that would have been worse..."

"Argh! The time!" Mama turns off the TV with a flick of the remote. "Ruth Kerril is a saint, boys. But right now, grab your school bags and let's go!"

JAMES

"Is Ruth a mar... mar...tyr like that man?" I ask, as we walk to school on either side of Mama.

Mama doesn't need to ask which man I mean. "Yes, James, she certainly is." She looks very serious as she goes on, "She must have loved the Lord a lot to hold firm like that. May we all do as well as her, in such a situation."

I don't know why, but for some reason her expression makes our father pop into my mind, and I've spoken without thinking. "Will our Dada ever come back, Mama?"

She flinches and the smile falls right off her face, the way it always does when our father is mentioned. "Oh James, why do you keep asking that? Perhaps I haven't made it clear enough. Your father's Muslim, and not a tolerant man."

"And he left when you found Jesus," says John. "Just before we were born. We know. But he could come back, couldn't he?"

"The only way *he'd* ever come back would be if he found Jesus too," says Mama, rather grimly, then adds under her breath, "And then he'd have to find *us*." She shakes her head. "Please try and forget about him, both of you. And don't go talking about it to anyone..."

"We know, we know." John rolls his eyes. "You don't want him to know where we are."

I sigh. Then I realize Mama's looking at me with that

unhappy expression we don't like to see on her face, like she feels she's let us down somehow. "It's okay," I say quickly. "We've got a father, haven't we? The Father. You can't beat that!"

Mama smiles. "Amen," she says.

TERESA

I close the door quietly, take off the council badge that says I'm safe to work with children and put it on the hall table, then tip-toe towards the stairs. April and June were no trouble, of course, but Thomas was really winding me up and the last thing I need is another argument with my dad...

Getting up to my room without mishap, I slump into my desk chair and turn on my computer. Check my emails. Check the news. A headline catches my eyes.

4 CHISBROOK SCHOOLGIRLS ON LONG WALK TO FREEDOM

It's been almost six months now since the kidnapping and I've heard nothing recently. I click on the article and read eagerly. Four more girls are free! Thank God! They escaped from a 'camp' somewhere in Albania and walked for seven days through the barren countryside to reach safety. Jessica, Mary, Shannon and Kettie are their names.

The rest isn't so good, though. Albanian troops sent immediately to search the area found a farm that showed signs of recent inhabitation—but there was no one there. Worse, the girls who escaped had been raped every day. Every day! I shiver. I can't even imagine that. The escapees also report that a total of four girls were killed on the journey from the UK. It gives their names as Yoko, Becky, Daniyah, and Ruth. Two girls have died from untreated snake bite—Josephine and Kris—and the men have killed several more for what they call 'disobedience', which apparently means anything from refusing to convert to

125

Islam, to trying to escape, to the men just feeling like it. The girls don't know the names of every girl killed in other 'camps', but said a girl called Georgie and a girl called Terri had been shot at the farm where they were.

Also, almost twenty girls were sick when they left, four of them seriously so. The four are named as Hannah, Carol, Grace and Sasha. The paper doesn't list the other eighteen, but I read all the names with great attention, though it hurts. It reminds me that they're real girls, my age. And despite the social media campaign, despite all the government's promises, despite the huge search, nothing's happened. They're being forgotten.

The government has got a lot on its plate, I know. There have been other kidnappings, killings, bombs... And our new Prime Minister is such a pacifist, he's not much use when it comes to this sort of thing. But still. How can two hundred and... now nineteen... teenage girls be abandoned to slavery?

I finish the article. It reminds us at the bottom that actually *al-Qabda* are keeping more like six hundred women of various ages as slaves in their secret camps.

Six hundred.

And what can *I* do about it?

I sit for a time. After a while it occurs to me to say a prayer. Eventually I get out my violin and play. When I'm satisfied, I write a couple of signs, because I'll be too shy to speak on camera, then start the webcam and hold each sign up for what I hope is long enough.

4 down, 219 to go.
#GetOurGirlsBack

This is for the 219,
and for the entire 600.

Then I pick up my violin, close my eyes so I can forget that the camera is rolling, and start to play. I play from the bottom of my soul, my own pain, my own grief, for the girls, for Mum, for the mess that is my relationship with my Dad, for everything that ails anyone in the world.

But mostly for the forgotten girls.

When I've finished I hold up each sign again, and then I post it online. This is the only thing I can do.

Other people have the same idea. Soon three very young—and oddly familiar—looking soldiers, two of them identical twins who look like they might be Muslim, post a video. They've made *two hundred and seventy-six* tiny plasticine figures, each with a head and limbs, they've drawn circles on pieces of paper, 'FREE', 'DEAD', 'CAPTIVE', and they each pick up a little figure, hold up their phones, each displaying a photo of one of the schoolgirls, then silently place the figure into the correct circle. And pick up the next, swiping to the next photo...

When they move the four new escapees from the remaining 'CAPTIVE' figures, one can hardly tell the difference. And even three at a time it takes a while for them to get through the rest. Each one placed right back into 'CAPTIVE'. They never say a word, and the photos and little 3D figures are kind of mesmerizing. Their video's going to get way more hits than mine. Deserves to, the amount of work they've put into it.

People still remember. But there's so little we can do.

So I go to Twitter and tweet:

@GOVUK—4 down, 219 to go. #GetOurGirlsBack

127

JUST BECAUSE IT ISN'T HAPPENING TO US (YET)
DOESN'T MEAN IT ISN'T HAPPENING

In the early hours of the 15th April 2014 the extremist Islamist group Boko Haram kidnapped 276 schoolgirls from Chibok school in Nigeria.

53 managed to escape by jumping from vehicles or by sneaking away from camps during the journey.

On 30th May 2014, local volunteer militia found 2 schoolgirls tied to a tree, half dead. They had been raped and left to die. The girls reported that 4 other girls had been killed for 'disobedience'.

Between April and October 2014, 102 other girls were kidnapped from other areas by Boko Haram, and hundreds of people were killed, 300 in one village alone.

In October 2014, 4 girls walked through the bush for three weeks to reach freedom. They said they had been raped every day in the camp.

219 schoolgirls remain captive.

It is believed that they have been forced to convert to Islam and that many have been sold in 'marriage' for $12.

In 2014, it was believed that Boko Haram were holding up to 600 women in their camps; by 2015, this had risen to 2000.

Since a major offensive against Boko Haram began in 2015, over 1000 women and girls have been reported to have been rescued.

None of the Chibok schoolgirls were among them.

At least another 1000 women and girls remain in captivity.

If we forget, then for them and many others, there is no hope at all that *someday* will ever come.

YESTERDAY & TOMORROW: 1

TOMORROW'S DEAD

It's a beautiful summer morning.
A normal day.

Teresa Seale is looking after a vulnerable child.
Alleluia Williams is setting off to Rome for Ruth Kerril's
beatification.
John and James Almara are on their way to school.
Sam Worthing is still in bed after a late night of essay-writing.
Isaar and Rishad Iqbal are making their breakfast.
Jasper Tregorian is foraging for his along the hedgerows.

Then their world changes forever in a haze of smoke and
gunfire.

Surrounded by black flags, they just want to survive.

But soon they must choose whether to be live cowards –
or risk becoming dead heroes.

READ A SNEAK PEEK ON P.161

Paperback: ISBN 978-1-910806-18-0
ePub: ISBN 978-1-910806-19-7

Find out more at: *www.YandT.co.uk*

NOTE FROM THE AUTHOR

"The blockade was up to 40 vehicles long. When the men in military uniform separated the Muslims from the Christians, we knew then they were Boko Haram. All young men including Muslims were told to either join the insurgents or be killed. They slit the throat of some of the men, saying they'd not waste bullets on them. Christian women wearing pants were shot in the leg and left to die. Older Muslim men and women wearing Muslim veils were released to go, while the rest of us were driven to their camp in Sambisa forest."

From 'Those Terrible Weeks in their Camp', Human Rights Watch *report on Boko Haram Violence against Women and Girls in Northeast Nigeria*

This is the account of a 20-year-old woman who was abducted by Boko Haram when she ran into a roadblock mounted by insurgents at Firgi, near Bama. This (in Nigeria at the time) commonplace event happened in May 2013, almost a year before the Chibok schoolgirls were kidnapped, and the activities of Boko Haram were catapulted into the world's consciousness.

I had been aware of the suffering of Christians and others in Nigeria for some time but the scale of the Chibok kidnapping could not but capture my attention, as it did that of the world. But as the days dragged into weeks, and then into months, with no real progress, and the world's interest began to wane again, I increasingly wished that there was something I could do to help. As an author, the obvious thing was to write the girls' story. But having never been to Africa, or made any in-depth study of the girls' culture, for some time I hesitated to embark on such a task.

Then I happened to re-watch *Save the Children's* Syria advert, probably one of the most powerful and effective I've ever seen. It still moves me to tears even though I've seen it many times. If you haven't watched it, just search for 'Save the Children Syria advert'. Using the format of a second a day video, the advert shows a year in the life of a little girl, during which she goes from happy normality, to the horrors of living through a civil war. But the genius of the advert is that the little girl is a white middle class British girl, and the location is London. With this simple switch, the advert strips away the buffer normally provided by cultural difference, and forces the viewer to empathize one hundred percent with what is happening.

As soon as I saw the advert again, I knew how to write my Chibok story in such a way that the reader cannot (I hope) simply turn away. I also really wanted to materially help those affected by the Boko Haram violence and I knew that donating to *Aid to the Church in Need* is a great way to do this, because they give a huge amount of support to Christians in Nigeria. However, I don't have a great deal of money, so it's a bit like in the Christmas carol, 'If I were a shepherd, I would give a lamb'. I'm an author, so I'm giving them a book!

Once I'd decided *how* to write it, I quickly realized that the novella would fit perfectly as a prequel to my new series, YESTERDAY & TOMORROW, in which I was already, less consciously, employing the location switch device, in that case setting similar events to those happening in Iraq and Syria in the UK. (To read the first chapter of book 1, TOMORROW'S DEAD, go to p. 161.)

Immediately following this afterword are some true stories from Chibok schoolgirls and others who have suffered at the hands of Boko Haram, and links to additional stories (including other first-hand accounts from Chibok escapees, which were not able to be reproduced here due to copyright issues). All the links can also be found on the website (www.YandT.co.uk). As you will see when you read the stories, I have kept the events of the novella as close to real life as was possible with the altered location. Most of the changes involve timings, and are a necessity of the much smaller distances involved in Europe as opposed to Africa.

I have made a few other small changes: for example, reports indicate that the four schoolgirls murdered during the journey were all shot; this is not the case with all four in the novella. Due to their interpretation of particular verses in the Quran, Islamist extremists consider throat-cutting a particularly fitting way to kill Christians and nonbelievers, and, as the quote above makes clear, frequently employ this method, hence I included it in the novella.

It would appear that the schoolgirls were split into small groups once they were deep in the forest, and taken to different locations. From the variety of experiences reported by escapees, it seems clear that exactly how badly girls are treated depends largely on the commander of their particular group. Many commanders have been reported to have made some effort to protect girls from sexual violence at least until they had been forcibly married off (See 'Human Rights Watch' Report, link on p. 159).

Monica Sunday, a woman who escaped from Boko Haram, reported meeting a group of twenty-four Chibok schoolgirls in a camp where she was held. She said that they were homesick and depressed, and being forced to perform manual work, but that they had not been physically injured, sexually abused, or forced to convert (See 'Monica Sunday,' link on p. 158). Yet stories from other escapees make it clear that in other camps, all these things have been happening (See most of the other stories). Even Monica Sunday reported that another woman in the camp was beaten until she converted to Islam, and she herself was placed under considerable pressure and terrorized in an attempt to make her convert. Boko Haram's own video seems to show girls having been forcibly converted to Islam.

Similarly, four girls were shot on the journey from Chibok for being uncooperative in some way, and others have been reported to have been shot in the camps for refusing to convert (See 'Baba Goni', p. 142)—yet three other girls are reported to have been released due to lack of space in the truck, despite one being a very firm and defiant Christian (See 'Saratu Isa', link on p. 158). The random nature of the mistreatment only makes it more chilling.

I have tried to reprint here only articles that seem to come from reliable sources. There are many far more horrific details to be read in articles from Nigerian websites. Two are particularly difficult to forget. The first is a report by a Pastor apparently running a trauma counselling program that has worked with some of the escaped schoolgirls, who reported that one of the girls had been raped 15 times a day by 15 different men. Although details are given about the pastor, his organization, and partner organizations, the story has not been picked up by any major news outlets, for which reason I have omitted it.

The second report is from a Nigerian Muslim Senator who said that he had heard (on the grapevine somehow) that some of the Chibok girls were being raped and then shot. He recounted how one girl had apparently begged on her knees to be allowed time to recover so that she could be raped again, out of fear that she would be shot like some of the others. Horrendous, but again, very hard to verify.

Thankfully, it's clear from reading the majority of the reports that such extremes of brutality (if true) are not the norm. However, even in the most positive description of the lives of a group of the kidnapped schoolgirls (See 'Monica Sunday,' link on p. 158–no abuse or forced conversion) we should never forget the horror of teenage girls being torn from their families, from the villages they may never have left before, to live in constant fear for two years as slaves to strangers, with no end in sight—no hope of regaining their freedom, let alone continuing their education. And even here, it's clear that other women in that camp have not been so lucky.

Baba Goni's story (p. 142), in particular, also reminds us that it's not only women and girls being abducted. Boys and young men are taken as well, while older men are often killed outright.

However, it's not all bad news from Nigeria. More recently, new president Muhammadu Buhari has made destroying Boko Haram one of the priorities of his presidency. A new offensive has scattered the Boko Haram fighters who once dominated vast areas of countryside.

Unfortunately, the group has continued to carry out atrocities even whilst on the run, like the one in February 2016, in the village of Dalori, where they burned homes, massacred civilians and abducted children. They are also continuing to use young captives as suicide bombers, such as the two girls who killed themselves and 58 people, wounding 78, at a camp for those fleeing Boko Haram violence in February 2016 (See 'Liberated Women and Girls', link on p. 159).

But this attack was apparently in revenge for an army attack on a Boko Haram market that killed 100 Boko Haram fighters. The revenge attacks are bad news—but the good news is that many Boko Haram camps have now been destroyed, and over a thousand women and girls have been freed over the last year. Sadly, none of the Chibok girls have been among them, and mass graves have been discovered where commanders have ordered their men to kill their 'wives' and sex slaves to prevent them from being liberated by advancing government troops.

Chillingly, many of the girls who have been freed have been pregnant as a result of forced marriages or sex slavery. Even worse, many are being rejected by their communities, who fear they may have been radicalized, or that their children have 'bad blood'. But at least they are free, and at least their innocent babies will be born into what is becoming, at the moment, a slightly safer Nigeria (See 'Liberated Women and Girls' and 'Um Haleema', links on p. 159).

There's a long way to go, especially for Christians, who are bearing the brunt of Boko Haram's onslaught. But some progress is finally being made. By buying this novella, you have helped support persecuted Christians in Nigeria and other countries. I would like to thank you and encourage you to follow the situation, and do what you can to help.

Please pray for the Chibok schoolgirls; all captives and victims of Boko Haram; and the Christians of Nigeria.

The following stories were first printed in a wide range of publications and are written by a wide range of authors. Their inclusion here in no way implies my endorsement of the views of the publication or the author, or of any of their other output.

TRUE STORIES

LAMI, MARIA & HAJARA

Lami, Maria and Hajara were at school in Chibok, north-eastern Nigeria, when they were kidnapped in April. Best friends Lami and Maria escaped by jumping from the back of a truck. Hajara was taken to a camp but later fled with another girl.

Lami: It was Monday night. We had exams the following day. Then we started to hear shootings in the town. So we went out. We phoned our parents to tell them what was happening in the town. They told us to run away when we got the chance. We told them that the town was already surrounded so there was no way we could run.

Maria: Lami woke me up saying: "Maria didn't you hear what's happening? Haven't you heard sounds of shooting from the town?" I said we should climb the wall and run away. She said: "No. No-one has run away. We should gather in one place and wait to see what's going to happen." Other girls said nothing would happen to us. "We're girls. They don't do anything to girls. We should wait and see what God would do."

Lami: We were at the school when suddenly three Boko Haram members entered. They said: "If any of you attempt to leave we'll kill all of you." When we went out they were everywhere. They gathered us where we have our school assembly. As we were there they kept burning the school. They burnt everything.

Hajara: They asked us to get out of the gate, saying that when we were out they would let us go back to our homes. They said whoever did not have a headscarf or shoes should go and get them. They then asked us to climb on to a lorry, on top of the food loaded in it. The lorry was so high that we couldn't easily climb on.

Maria: They said to us: "You're only coming to school for prostitution. Boko (Western education) is haram (forbidden) so what are you doing in school?" We kept quiet. I think there could have been about 100 Boko Haram members - they were all over the school. They outnumbered us. They took us away in their vehicles. We were sitting on oil drums in the vehicle. Our vehicle was really overloaded. We were saying to one another that we should throw away our shoes and scarves so that if our parents came they would know the road we had taken.

Hajara: The vehicle became full before I could get on. There were about 100 of us walking. We stopped at one town and people brought us water. I saw one of those who brought us water changed his clothes and joined the Boko Haram men. They then put us in other vehicles. They put the rest in the boots of cars. Some of the Boko Haram members were so small that if I were to grab their necks I could break them. Some couldn't even carry their guns properly.

Maria: We were wondering where we were being taken to. When we entered the vehicle, Lami said to me: "Shouldn't we jump out of the vehicle here so that we may possibly escape? There are no other vehicles close by."

Hajara: I thought, it's preferable to have these people shoot me as I run than have them humiliate me. They kept saying to us: "Make sure you put on your scarves. Make sure you put on your scarves. We'll shoot any girl we see without a scarf. And any girl who jumps out will die." I was about to jump out when one girl held me back and said they'd shoot me if I did. "What's the difference," I said. "Is it not to the same death we're going? They should shoot me here and let my corpse be collected." I was crying and praying until we reached the camp.

Lami: There was a lot of dust on the road, they couldn't see us. When we jumped out, we started to run. We were running without shoes. We found other people. We started to run away from them thinking they were Boko Haram. But they too had run from the town.

Hajara: Boko Haram gathered us in a forest around noon. Some of the girls were tired and were lying down. But I couldn't lie down. The spirit of God was asking me to go. It was telling me: "Get up and go. Get up and go." So I went. Another girl followed me. When we were going I saw some of them [Boko Haram members] performing ablutions. We stooped as if we were trying to pull out thorns from our shoes, as if we were just going to wee. We'd walk a little then bend down for a little while as if we were looking for something we'd lost. After walking for a while they couldn't see us properly since it was forest. We then started to run. After we had run for a short distance, we heard them saying "catch those girls." We kept running. Whether they came after us not, we didn't know.

Hajara: We kept going and our shoes were ripped. We found a house, where a girl could speak Hausa. Her parents gave us a place to sleep. We reached the Chibok area in the morning. A man looking for a relative among the missing girls drove us on motorbike into town. When I saw my elder and younger brothers, I fell to the ground crying. My mother and father were crying and all members of my family cried. Before I reached home it was as if there was a death in the house. Mats were spread. People were consoling my father and mother thinking that I had died.

Lami: The people we met said: "Your town is far away. You can't go there now. Come here and wait until morning when we'll take you into the town to get transport back home." We stayed there till morning when they asked us to get up so that we go to the town. We couldn't walk. Our feet were full of thorns. They said: "Let's go find a vehicle to take you home."

Maria: The men who helped us took us to Chibok, and I cried. It was the second time that something like that had happened to me. My dad was a pastor; Boko Haram went to our house and killed him. They also shot my mum in the stomach.

Lami: My parents warmed up water and cared for my feet. I was taken to the hospital and it was two weeks before I could stand up.

Maria: I continued to live with the thought that Boko Haram members were coming to get me. I couldn't sleep.

Hajara: I was having nightmares every day. There was even a day when I dreamed that they gathered all of us who fled in one place, and said to us: "You girls have defied us and fled. We're now going to burn you alive." I haven't forgotten about the other girls who are still in the hands of those people. I keep praying for them.

Lami: God will never make us meet these people again. And for our sisters who are still in the forest, may God help them.

And may the whole world cry out for these girls to get out so that we continue with our education in school again.

Maria: They should pray to God to forgive them their sins. I'd also ask them to bring back the girls they have kidnapped because their parents are in distress. Some of the parents of the girls have already died. It was the thought of their girls that killed them.

Hajara: God will do what he wills, but I don't want to look at them because of what they have done to my life. They think they've ruined me, but God willing, they haven't ruined me. I'll continue with my education.

This is a transcript of an interview broadcast on the *BBC's* '100 Women' programme, published on 27th October 2014. The girls' names have been changed for their protection.

BABA GONI

Their faces scratched and bleeding, the pitiful remains of their once-smart school uniforms ripped and filthy, the two teenage girls were tethered to trees, wrists bound with rope and left in a clearing in the Nigerian bush to die by Islamist terror group Boko Haram.

Despite having been raped and dragged through the bush, they were alive—but only just—in the sweltering tropical heat and humidity.

This grim scene was discovered by 15-year-old Baba Goni. "They were seated on the ground at the base of the trees, their legs stretched out in front of them—they were hardly conscious," says Baba, who acted as a guide for one of the many vigilante teams searching for the Nigerian schoolgirls abducted from their school last month by Boko Haram—and now at the centre of a concerted international campaign for their freedom.

The horrific scene he and his comrades encountered, a week after the kidnap early on April 15, was in thorny scrubland near the village of Ba'ale, an hour's drive from Chibok, where 276 girls aged 16 to 18 were taken from their boarding school dormitories—with 223 still missing. It was still two weeks before social media campaigns and protests would prick the Western world's conscience over the abduction.

In the days following their disappearance, rag-tag groups such as Baba's, scouring the forests in a convoy of Toyota pick-up trucks, were the girls' only hope.

But hope had already run out for some of the hostages, according to Baba, when his group spoke to the terrified inhabitants of the village where Boko Haram had pitched camp with their captives for three days following the kidnap.

The chilling account he received from the villagers, though unconfirmed by official sources, represents the very worst fears of the families of those 223 girls still missing.

Four were dead, they told him, shot by their captors for being 'stubborn and uncooperative'. They had been hastily buried before the brutish kidnappers moved on.

"Everyone we spoke to was full of fear," said Baba. "They didn't want to come out of their homes. They didn't want to show us the graves. They just pointed up a track."

The tiny rural village, halfway between Chibok and Damboa in the besieged state of Borno in Nigeria's north-east, had been helpless to stop the Boko Haram gang as it swept through on trucks loaded with schoolgirls they had taken at gunpoint before torching their school.

Venturing further up the track, Baba and his fellow vigilantes found the two girls. Baba, the youngest of the group, stayed back as his friends took charge. "They used my knife to cut through the ropes," he said. "I heard the girls crying and telling the others that they had been raped, then just left there. They had been with the other girls from Chibok, all taken from the school in the middle of the night by armed men in soldiers' uniforms.

"We couldn't do much for them. They didn't want to talk to any men. All we could do was to get them into a vehicle and drive them to the security police at Damboa. They didn't talk, they just held on to each other and cried."

For Baba, a peasant farmer's son who has never been out of rural Borno, it was shocking to see young girls defiled and brutalized by the notorious terrorists he knew so well.

But his own life has been full of tragedy and he told how he had 'seen much worse' than the horror of that day in the forest clearing.

A bright-eyed Muslim boy from the Kanuri ethnic group, proud of a tribal facial scar and nicknamed 'Small' by all who know him because of his short, slim frame, he described a happy childhood with three brothers and two sisters in Kachalla Burari, a collection of mud houses not far from Chibok.

Without electricity or running water, the children spent their days helping on their father's subsistence farm, planting maize and beans and millet.

Baba and his friends used home-made catapults to shoot birds and in the rainy season fished in the river with bent hooks. But by his tenth birthday, the scourge of the radical Islamist Boko Haram was creeping up on everyone in Borno State.

Baba and his siblings attended a local madrassa, or religious school, where they learnt the Quran, but he had no formal teaching and cannot read or write to this day.

By 2009, Boko Haram were becoming active in his area, peddling their message of hatred to Christians, but also turning on Muslims they branded as informers. Nigeria's chaotic military was incapable of defending itself or its citizens.

Baba's village life came under siege. There were attacks on the Christian population in the region, with bank robberies funding the gang. Disaffected, unemployed youths from local families were recruited and neighbours who once lived in peace now spied on one another.

One night as he slept in his family's mud house in the village, the gunmen came door to door, looking for informers. "I heard some noise, I woke up and saw men coming through the door, shooting at my uncle who was in the bed beside mine," he said. "That was the end of my childhood, the end of everything. I saw his body covered in blood, I backed away, and the men turned their guns on me. They grabbed me roughly and took me

144

outside to a pick-up truck."

Baba, telling his story confidently and lucidly, wants to skate over the details of his two hellish years in the Boko Haram camp in Sambisa Forest. Today there are special forces soldiers swarming over the vast nature reserve and circling overhead in surveillance aircraft.

For this slight boy, there was no such worldwide interest as he scurried back and forth at the command of a ruthless gang dug into woodland far from any help or rescue.

He remembers many of them lived with women who had come voluntarily into the camp. He never saw any girls abducted. This latest phenomenon is unknown to him. "There were many abducted boys, but no girls," he said. "We were all scared to death and had to do whatever we were told—fetch water, fetch firewood, clean the weapons.

"We couldn't make friends—you didn't know who to trust. I was made to sleep next to the Boko Haram elders, the senior preachers. I had no special boss in the camp, I was ordered around by everybody."

The men prayed five times a day yet would leap on their motorbikes and trucks to carry out killing sprees.

"I knew they had started out as holy men but now I saw them as criminals, loaded with weapons and ammunition," he said.

As he got older, he was taught how to use an AK-47, how to strip it down and clean it, and reassemble it.

He could never understand what drove the men. They did not use alcohol or hard drugs, though he sometimes saw them smoking marijuana. They were monsters and he felt convinced they were mad.

"They were wild, even when they prayed so loudly in groups together, making us join in. They were insane, unpredictable, and always planning their next attack. I never wanted to be one of them.

"They slept rough every night, just taking shelter under trees in the rainy season," he said. "We all wore the same *afaraja* [the Nigerian long shift and trousers] day and night. We washed them when we could. We slept on mats made of palm leaves, out in the open with the trucks all parked nearby, ready for a hasty move if necessary."

He said the fear, and the endless boredom, were his worst enemies. "They made us work hard so it was easy to sleep. I don't remember crying through homesickness. I think the night when my uncle was killed in front of me did something to my feelings forever. It seems mindless, but I adapted to my life out there."

Then came the day when he was given a 'special' but sickening task. One of the commanders told him he was going on a journey and would be tested for his loyalty to the group.

"He brought two of his senior men to stand beside me. He said I would be going with them to my family's home and I would have to shoot and kill my father." Baba had no time to plan. He was sandwiched between the two fanatics as they set off on a motorbike for his village home.

"I pretended I was willing to do the job. I took the ammunition belt I was handed and clung on as we drove through the rough bush. When we were less than a mile from a nearby village, I threw the ammunition belt to the ground and pretended it had slid out of my hands.

"They stopped to let me pick it up. Instead, I ran as fast as I could through the undergrowth. I didn't care about thorns or snakes or anything. They shot at me and I could hear the bullets flying past and hitting the trees, but I was not going to stop for anything. I made it to the village and some kind people let me hide there.

"The shooting would have been heard by local vigilante groups. I think that is why I wasn't followed by the men on the bike."

The next day Baba went home. He saw his grieving parents and siblings for the first time in two years.

"But I couldn't stay," he said. "I was bringing danger to their door and we all knew it."

Confirmation of that came when Baba soon heard that vengeful Boko Haram chiefs had put a bounty on his head for his defiance of the equivalent of £12,000—a fortune in the local economy.

"I took a bus to Damboa, to report to the youth vigilante group," he said. "I wanted to work with them and I knew I was doing the right thing."

His family, terrified, abandoned their home soon afterwards and today live in a remote part of Borno, rarely seeing their eldest son. He lives with a cousin who is also under a Boko Haram death threat.

He became a valuable volunteer with the vigilantes. He helps man checkpoints where Baba points out members of Boko Haram to the rest of the team.

But he was soon exposed to brutality of a different kind—this time from the government side. He helped to get one of his captors, a man he only knew as Alaji, arrested and handed to the soldiers.

"It felt good at first, but then they shot him dead right in front of me," he said.

Now joining the patrols armed with a shotgun and machete, Baba has been able to give valuable intelligence to the Nigerian authorities about Boko Haram's way of life in their camps.

"By now I have seen this violence many times. It never gets better. It will always be an even worse sight than finding those poor schoolgirls in the forest," he says.

This article was written by **Barbara Jones** and first appeared in *The Mail on Sunday* on 18th May 2014.

CHIBOK GIRLS WHO WALKED TO FREEDOM

Four kidnapped Chibok schoolgirls escaped a Boko Haram camp in Cameroon, raising hopes for the more than 200 still missing. Boko Haram operates along the border with Cameroon, and the violence frequently spills over it.

The four girls, all aged between 16 and 18, had been told that if they criticized Boko Haram, their families would be killed. They were helped to escape by a teenage boy, also a prisoner, who managed to get them out of the camp, according to Stephen Davis, a British-Australian negotiator who had tried to bargain with the extremist Islamic group for the schoolgirls' freedom.

The four free girls walked west for three weeks guided by the setting sun, finally arriving in a Nigerian village, starving and traumatized.

"They were amazing—to first escape and then walk for weeks. They are the only ones that have escaped from a Boko Haram camp," Mr Davis, who used to be the canon emeritus of Coventry Cathedral, said.

Mr Davis has now abandoned his attempts at negotiation after realizing that if the girls from the town of Chibok were freed, Boko Haram would just kidnap more girls. Instead, he is trying to cut the militants off financially, by persuading Britain, America and other countries to freeze the bank accounts of high-profile Nigerians who are allegedly channelling money to them.

This is part of an article written by Ruth Maclean, which first appeared in *The Times* on 12th October 2014.

LADI APAGU

Boko Haram entered Sabon Gari village about 7 p.m. We heard gunshots. The shots sounded like thunder, so the children were jumping and smiling and singing, "Let the rain come, let the rain come." But I realised it was not thunder.

Boko Haram fighters were everywhere. We saw them on the motorbikes shooting and burning houses. All night, the sound of guns shooting was in the air. They left in the morning. I was so scared, but I didn't have anywhere else to go, so I stayed.

After the fourth attack, I decided to leave Sabon Gari because I know Boko Haram likes to kidnap girls [Ladi was 16 at the time]. I went to Gulak to live with my great-aunt. Later I learned that Boko Haram attacked Sabon Gari a fifth time.

Then in September, Boko Haram came to Gulak. As soon as I heard the gunshots, I told my great aunt that I am leaving Gulak. The old woman became sad, and she asked me to stay with her because she is old and did not want to be left by herself. I told her that I cannot stay because Boko Haram kidnaps girls my age. She understood, so I fled. I ran, joined by a Muslim woman who was a distant relative. As we were running, we saw a soldier behind us. At first, we were alarmed. We thought it was a Boko Haram member wearing a soldier uniform. But the soldier told us not to worry, that he is also running away from Boko Haram.

The woman and I fled into the bush and spent about a week sleeping and eating there. It was uncomfortable, and I suffered.

I hated staying in the bush, especially when it rained. I decided it was better to leave the bush, even if Boko Haram killed me. So the woman and I ran to a mountain. At night, it was cold. And after a few days living there, Boko Haram came very close to where we were staying. We escaped and went to a house we saw in another village.

We stayed with a Muslim family there for some days, but then we heard Boko Haram fighters. They were coming fast, so we all ran away. The family told us they were going to Gulak. They told me to join them there, but I told them that Boko Haram fighters are inside Gulak. They told me that they would protect me because they are Muslims with good knowledge of the Quran, so Boko Haram will not harm them. I decided to follow them, but Boko Haram was still shooting in the street, and I somehow lost the Muslim family. I kept running, looking for them, but I could not find them. So I joined some women on the street who were also running toward Gulak.

In Gulak I found the Muslim family who had taken care of me. They told me I need to leave because Boko Haram is going around, killing people who are not Muslims.

So I left. I didn't know where to go, but I knew I just had to run. In my confusion, I bumped into some young Christian girls. We went to hide in the mountains and heard many gunshots. We could not detect where the gunshots were coming from because the mountains made the sound of gunshots echo. I was so confused. We ran down the mountain, and we got lost. And that's how we ended back up in Gulak. Right away, a Boko Haram member saw me and told me to stop running. He threatened to shoot my legs, but the other Boko Haram member with him said it is not good to shoot women.

I asked them where are they taking me to. They told me they are taking me to a place where I will worship Allah. In Gulak they drove to a big house that was surrounded by a barbed wire fence. When I entered the house, I saw many other girls who were close to my age. They, too, had been abducted. I saw some of the Christian girls I met in the mountains.

Boko Haram members asked if we will convert to Islam, and we said no. There were some girls who did agree to convert, so the insurgents separated those who agreed to convert and those who did not. They held a big knife up to my neck and asked me, "You do not want to convert to Islam? We will kill you along with this retired soldier we captured over there who also refuses to convert." So I finally said, "Yes, I will convert." I begged them not to kill me.

They brought out one man who they said they had captured from a neighbouring village. They put him on the ground. The man begged for his life. Then the insurgents set their flag behind the man and slaughtered him right in front of us girls.

There were many Boko Haram fighters in that house. They had long hair, which they brush down and pack it into three long braids. They were very dirty. Some of them wore turbans on their heads. They were speaking many languages—Kanuri, Arabic, Hausa and Fulani.

I stayed in that house from October until January. Every day, we had to pray five times and read our Quranic studies, but I would often forget to do so. Whenever they found me not praying or studying the Quran, they would beat me and the other girls, 10 lashes each. If we did not wake up early enough in the morning to pray, they poured cold water on us. One day, they dragged out one girl who refused to pray, pulling her in front of us so we could see them shout at her. They said they will take her to Madagali town, to a place that they call their prison. The girl disappeared, and for six days we never saw her. When they returned, she had changed. She did her prayers and Quranic studies without complaint.

I was suffering so much. We saw the women that the Boko Haram members use as cooks in another part of the house. Sometimes the women would pity us and sneak us extra food.

Every day, more girls arrived in the house from other towns that Boko Haram had attacked. They kept kidnapping women and girls. The number of girls I shared a bedroom with kept growing, from 10 to 20 to 30. It's a very big house.

As for the prayers, I just didn't want to do it. I would lie and tell them I am menstruating, so I cannot pray. But the Boko Haram leaders knew I was lying so they would beat me. One day, the boy who teaches us the Quran—his name was Adamu Yusuf—beat me so bad that I had bloody bruises all over my legs. I was crying. The Boko Haram leader of the house heard me crying, and he called me by the new name they had given me, Fatima. He asked, "Fatima why are you crying?" I told him that Adamu Yusuf had beat me. The leader scolded Adamu and said he should not beat women and girls. He said they are to do the work of God and beating people like this is not good.

But Adamu Yusuf liked to beat us. He even beat a pregnant woman. The Boko Haram leader was so angry, and he shouted at Adamu that pregnant women should not be maltreated. He said, "Pregnant women are our mothers. If you beat them, God will surely punish you, because we are to do the work of God."

That's how they kept us there in that house. I think there were about 200 women and girls there. They kept us under heavy guard, especially the younger girls like me.

Then one day in December, they told us we will soon be getting married. We cried and pleaded. The Boko Haram fighters became angry and asked us why are we crying. They said we are still behaving like infidels who refuse to marry their strong fighters. They told us, "Who do you think you are? Are you too good to get married to us? We are doing the work of God."

They called us into a room one afternoon and introduced us one by one to some of the Boko Haram fighters. They introduced me to a guy they call "One Arab," because he looked like an Arab man. His hair was long, and he had light skin. My other friends Zeinab—who was born with the name Sarah—Katturah and Maryam were also led to meet some of the men there. Maryam was to be married to Maman. Katturah was supposed to marry Mallam Ramat. And Zeinab was given to Direban Sambisa. We called him Sambisa because he was always driving back and forth to the Sambisa Forest. Sambisa is where Boko Haram has their main camp.

The Boko Haram fighters asked me, "Do you see this man, 'One Arab'?" I said yes. They said, "You will marry him in a few weeks' time. We will marry all of you off." We fell down and started crying and pleading to them. We told them we are not ready to get married. They started shouting at us. The leader came and told us it is final, we will get married, and we should stop crying because we are not better than them. He asked us, "Do you think you are better than those Chibok girls that we kidnapped?" He said the Chibok girls are enjoying their matrimonial homes. He said the Chibok girls have accepted the message of Boko Haram and have turned against their parents. He said the Chibok girls are ready to slit their parents' throats if they ever see them again. He told us we must accept true Islam because even the Chibok girls have accepted the religion. Then he told us to stop crying or they will kill us.

He said, "Fatima, wherever you go, even if you run all the way to Yola, we will run after you and kill you." He said I can never escape. Then he started talking about President [Goodluck] Jonathan, and he said Jonathan is an infidel and that they will slit his throat.

By that time, my friends and I were planning our escape. Many other girls had tried to escape, but they were always caught at the gate.

They would not let us go anywhere. We tried to ask them if

we can go out into the bush to look for vegetables to cook soup, but they refused. They said girls from our tribe have long legs and we run fast so they will not be able to catch us if we escape.

One day, some of the girls made food. I was in the bedroom when I heard the Boko Haram guards ask for some. They said girls from our tribe are good cooks. So the girls gave food to the guards, and the guards fell asleep. As they slept, the girls went to get a blanket to throw over the barbed wire fence. They climbed up a ladder and jumped over the fence. That's how they escaped.

But the guards woke up and realized what happened. The guards were so angry. They asked us what did the girls put in the food that made them fall asleep. I said I didn't know.

They went outside the compound looking for the girls, and they returned with the pregnant one. She told me she could not run fast enough because of her pregnancy, so she asked a woman in a village down the road to shelter her. Boko Haram went to the house and asked the woman if she is hiding anyone there. The woman said yes, and Boko Haram grabbed her.

The Boko Haram men told her she cannot go anywhere and the child she is carrying in her womb belongs to them.

When the pregnant woman returned to the house, she became so obedient and would always follow Boko Haram's instructions. They were very pleased with her behaviour and her excellence in studying the Quran. So they gave her some money and took her out of the compound. I never saw her again.

There was one day, I was not feeling well. My body was aching, and I became ill. The Boko Haram people brought their doctor, and the doctor connected me to a drip and gave me four injections. I started to feel better. I decided it was my time to escape. It was getting nearer to the wedding day, and I wanted to leave the house.

Me, a girl named Janet, another girl named Hassana and another named Hadja went to the well to fetch water. We told the other girls in the house that we want to wash our clothes. Then we wore a full veil, the one that only exposes the eyes—

153

the *niqab*. We wanted to try to look like Boko Haram's wives, because they wear a *niqab*. We took our clothes and tied some of them around our bodies so we can have a change of clothes. We disguised these clothes under the *niqab* to make it appear as if we were carrying babies on our backs.

The guards were not around, so we quickly threw a blanket over the barbed wire, climbed up the fence and jumped. We were finally outside the compound!

We walked out and saw some Boko Haram members standing by the roadside. They greeted us with "*Assalamu alaikum.*" We responded with "*Wa alaikum assalam.*" They asked, "Who are you?" We told them, "We are the wives of the *rijale*"—the strong men, because that is how the Boko Haram refer to themselves. So they allowed us to pass.

As we walked along, one of the girls became worried and said we will get caught and get killed. She pleaded for us to go back to the house. We said no. We told her the Boko Haram members will not remove our veils to check our faces. So we continued trekking. We saw an old man, and we asked him how to get to Cameroon. He showed us the way.

As we walked, we saw so many destroyed villages, burned-down houses, rotting corpses. We even saw cracked tombstones at graveyards and overturned coffins. We saw another set of old people. They asked us where are we going. We told them we are looking for the road to Cameroon. The old people pointed to the road to Cameroon, and they told us not to remove our *niqab* until we reach a village called Palam. They said once we reach Palam, we must take off our *niqab* because the villagers there will kill us because they will suspect we are from Boko Haram. They advised us to avoid the main road and go through the guinea cornfields.

So we walked through farm fields, and the sun was burning. We were sweating in the *niqab*, and the prickly grasses kept getting caught on our fabric. We were too tired. Then we saw a Boko Haram man driving toward us on a motorbike. He was carrying a machete. We ran so fast but he was after us, yelling, "I will kill you. You are the type of people who will report us in

Yola."

The man's motorbike skidded off the road, and he tumbled off but started running after us. Hassana, the oldest of us, shouted to keep running and not look back. I couldn't keep up, so I stopped to hide under some leaves. I dropped the clothes I had placed on my back, my Christian baptismal card and my photographs. The Boko Haram man who was chasing us couldn't find us, and we heard him stop. We were lucky he did not have a gun, or else he would have just shot us.

We saw some women sitting by the roadside in Palam, and we asked them to show us how to get to Cameroon. They asked us where were we coming from. We lied and told them we were living in the mountains and ran out of food. We asked the women if we can remove our *niqab*. They told us not to remove it because some Muslims living in the area will notice and will alert Boko Haram. We left the women, and after some time, I removed the *niqab*, but my friends kept theirs on. We saw a Christian woman roasting groundnuts, and she asked, "Who are you?" We told her that we had escaped from those people. She pointed at the road to Cameroon, and we continued. The *niqab* became too heavy for my friends, so they took off their *niqab* and handed it over to some old women we saw standing by a tree. It was night time.

We reached a village called Palam B and saw so many burned houses and a burned church. My friends and I decided to sleep in Palam B. We entered a compound and saw a Muslim family praying. We decided not to stay with a Muslim family, so we left. We saw a Christian woman, and we asked if we can stay with her. She refused. We asked her if there is anyone around from Gulak. She told us to go farther down the road and we will see a woman from Gulak.

We soon saw a woman from Gulak, and she gave us a room to sleep in. She said villagers in Palam B have been anxious because new Boko Haram recruits in the village had delivered a letter from Boko Haram threatening to kill them.

We stayed with her for two days, until she told us we had to leave because she learned that Boko Haram knew we were in the town because of the *niqab* that we had given to the women on the street.

She told us to run straight to Cameroon and not to pass through a village called Sina, because villagers there will kill us once they realize we had lived with Boko Haram.

We left, and on our way, we met a man who asked us if we had cellphones. I was the only one. But Boko Haram had deleted everything that had been in my phone, including all the Christian songs I had saved. They put in their own war chants and messages.

The man advised me to throw away the phone. He warned us that farther down the road, we might meet some people who will strip us naked and search us. If they find anything on us that looks like it came from Boko Haram, they will kill us.

Moving toward the Cameroonian border, we did not see a single person. We were all alone, surrounded by more burned houses and churches.

Then we saw a Muslim woman resting under a tree with her children. She told us that she fled from Michika and is on her way to Cameroon but will return to Nigeria to join her husband in the city of Jos. My friends and I accompanied the woman and her children to Cameroon. We arrived at the border on a Tuesday, and there some teenage boys harassed us, saying we cannot enter until we give them money. We explained to them that we are running for our lives and we don't have money. The boys blocked our way and said if we don't give them money, they will report us to the Cameroonian soldiers. The Muslim woman gave money to the boys, and we were allowed to enter Cameroon. We slept in the street because the people were not friendly and they did not want to help.

When we woke up, we decided to leave Cameroon, but Zeinab was still suffering from a leg injury she got when we jumped over the fence from the Boko Haram house in Gulak. Her leg was swollen, and we had to leave her. We told the Muslim woman that we are leaving. She blessed us, bought food for us to eat and then gave us 500 naira. She helped us to try to get a ride to Mubi, but none of the drivers were willing to take us there. So we told her goodbye, and we walked several kilometres to Mubi.

In the market there I met a girl I used to know from Sabon Gari. She was so happy to see me. I told her my story, and she gave me money for my friends and me to pay for transportation. Later we heard that Boko Haram is on its way to Mubi. Everyone in the town began to panic. We searched for a ride, but there was no room in anyone's car. So we gathered along with other people who were walking, and we walked until we reached a town called Maiha. I went to a parking lot to look for a vehicle to take us to Yola and heard someone call me by my native name.

I looked and saw a man I used to know in Sabon Gari. He asked me why I looked so dirty and tired. I told him everything that happened, and he took my friends and me to his home to meet his wife and children. They took care of us. They, too, had been displaced by Boko Haram. He gave me money for transportation, and on Jan. 18, my friends and I were in a car on the way to Yola.

My friends and I sat on the road once we arrived in Yola. We were not used to the city, and we were confused. I saw a girl who I know from home, and she was excited to see me. She told me that I have an uncle who is staying at St Theresa's Catholic Church. I went to the church, and now I am safe.

Ladi Apagu told her story to **Chika Oduah** in January 2015, and it was translated from Hausa, at St Theresa's Catholic Church in Yola. It has been edited for length. Ladi Apagu has since been relocated away from the northeast out of fear that Boko Haram members will come after her.

OTHER STORIES

KUMA ISHAKU, JOY BISHARA & GODIYA SIMON
(Chibok schoolgirls) told their stories in an article entitled,
'Tales of Escapees in Nigeria Add to Worries About Other
Kidnapped Girls' by Adam Nossiter, published in *The New York
Times* on 14th May 2014. I really, really wanted to reprint their
stories here because I drew a lot on them for the novella.
Unfortunately, due to copyright issues, I had to leave them out.
Google the title or find it here: *http://tinyurl.com/zup52fe*

SARATU ISA, RAHAB YAYA & COMFORT AYUBA
(Chibok schoolgirls) give first-hand accounts of their escapes in
the 'Chibok Affair' section of an article entitled 'Nigeria: Escape
from Boko Haram: We went through hell to survive—Chibok
Schoolgirls' by Sam Eyoboka, published on *Vanguard* on 2nd
August 2014. Find it here: *http://tinyurl.com/h7dncen*

ABIGAIL JOHN & DORCAS AIDEN, aged 15 and 20,
describe how they were kidnapped, held by Boko Haram, and
managed to escape, in a video and transcript entitled 'Nigeria
Chibok Girls' first published by *Associated Press* on February 11th
2015. Find it here: *http://tinyurl.com/hty2x8k*

MONICA SUNDAY, aged 20, describes how she was
kidnapped with her baby and held in a camp with some of the
Chibok schoolgirls for three days. She later managed to escape,
but her baby died. This article was written by Jonathan Miller
and first appeared on *Channel 4 News* on 12th February 2015.
Find it here: *http://tinyurl.com/hpw7zbv*

VICTORIA YOUHANA, aged 15, was kidnapped with her
mother and five brothers from Baga. They later managed to
escape, and Victoria came to the UK at the invitation of *Aid to
the Church in Need* to tell her story, which was published in the
Daily Express. You can read it here: *http://tinyurl.com/hr7gavy*

ANONYMOUS WOMEN AND GIRLS

In 2014 Human Rights Watch published a detailed report concerning the treatment of Women and Girls by Boko Haram. It is entitled *Those Terrible Weeks in their Camp: Boko Haram Violence against Women and Girls in Northeast Nigeria'* and it is well worth reading. It can be found here: *http://tinyurl.com/h6amc37*

There is also an excellent summary of the report by Radhika Sanghani entitled, 'Inside Boko Haram: Where women persuade men to rape kidnapped young girls', which first appeared in *The Telegraph* on 27th October 2014. Find it here: *http://tinyurl.com/zxqs5ma*

LIBERATED WOMEN AND GIRLS

Girls liberated from Boko Haram face rejection amid fears that they may have been radicalised and that their babies, fathered by Boko Haram fighters, will have 'bad blood'. Read more in this article by Dionne Searcey which first appeared in *The New York Times* on 16th February 2016: *http://tinyurl.com/zkvukou*

UM HALEEMA, a sixteen-year-old victim of a forced marriage to a Boko Haram man, was determined to keep her baby despite facing threats from her own Muslim community. See the article 'Boko Haram kidnap victim: Stigmatized for carrying captor's baby' by Nima Elbagir, first published on *CNN* on 11th June, 2015: *http://tinyurl.com/gsbapvk*

Links to all of the stories, plus additional ones, can be found at: *www.YandT.co.uk.*

TOMORROW'S DEAD

SNEAK PEEK

TERESA

"Look, look, Resa! Bird! Bird!" Thomas rushes up, shrieking with excitement and narrowly missing a tree.

"Thomas!" I'm too tired to spare more than a glance for the apparently bird-shaped rock. "Would you *please* keep it down? Every Quab in the country will hear you!"

Thomas turns to show his rock to Isaar, grabbing his arm with such enthusiasm Isaar only just stops his rifle swinging and bashing him. Isaar is predictably much more appreciative about the rock, but Thomas looks back to me at my words. "Quabs bad?"

"Yes, very bad. You know that."

"Why?" His favourite word.

"They do bad things to people. They'll do bad things to us if they catch us. You know that too."

"Why?"

Isaar sees my ragged look and answers for me. "They're... they're extremely ...deluded... people."

"What's *looded?*"

"It means, ah..."

Rishad leans around his twin, dark eyes flashing. "They're evil bastards doing the bidding of Shaitan, tell it as it is, Isaar."

"Rish!" I protest. "I'd like to give him back to his mum and dad with a larger vocabulary, *yeah,* but..."

Thomas isn't interested in *that* word, though—probably heard it already. "What's shay–ta?"

"Oh. Do you know who the devil is?"

Thomas frowns. "Bad?"

"Yes, all bad things come from the devil. Rish and Isaar call the devil by a different name, that's all. They call him Shaitan." Better not mention that's what the Quabs use too, that would really confuse him...

"Quab men devil men?"

"That's basically what Rish said, yes, and I won't argue with it."

"Who could," mutters Isaar.

"Very bad men." Thomas nods firmly to himself and

163

rushes off to the ends of his reins again. I ignore the familiar yank on my hand and keep walking. Sam looks my way in the twilight and smiles. I smile back, warmth in my stomach... eventually realize he's holding out a hand, offering to take Thomas for a while... I wave the offer away. He's enough to do being in command of this make-shift platoon.

"I've been meaning to ask," says Isaar, dropping his hand as though he'd been about to make the same offer as Sam, "what is Thomas's condition, specifically?"

"Well, it's called Global Development Delay, and that's really all I know. It's basically what it says." I watch the healthy looking seven-year-old boy charging around on the end of the baler twine reins. "His development's delayed. So his balance still isn't great and in some ways he's got the mental age of a... I don't know... three, four-year-old? Really wish I'd found out more, now that... well, y'know."

Isaar nods, eyes following Thomas affectionately as we climb out of a hollow, but also with a spark of more professional interest. Hmm. A third year medical student probably can't tell me much... but I might as well ask.

"Do you know what..."

CRACK...

Isaar staggers back, a glimpse of his shocked face and he crumples, falling back into the hollow. For a moment I'm too stunned to do anything but stare down at him... blood is spreading over his t-shirt... *Gunshot*...

I yank on the reins, bringing Thomas stumbling into me, and throw us both down beside Isaar. The shot came from ahead... if we stay down...

Sam's bellowing military things like, "Contact, *contact!*" "Down, get *down!*" "Return fire, *return fire!*" The guys are throwing themselves down behind trees and bushes and stones and *anything*... Guns are going off all around... Thomas clamps his hands over his ears, his mouth open in a silent scream, but he's still flat on the ground so I scramble to Isaar's side.

Rishad is already there, looking closer to panic than I've ever seen him. "Isaar! *Isaar!*"

Isaar's eyes are open, but shocked and uncomprehending—blood is bubbling and trickling from his mouth. My heart gives a terrified lurch—in films blood from the mouth always indicates imminent death...

No! No. I have to do something...

"Bandage!" I grab Rishad by the shoulders and yell it into his face. Even as I do I remember Sam telling me they didn't have many medical supplies, but they had a few proper bandages, stored in the top breast pocket—and Isaar has one because he's medic.

Oh no, Isaar's the only one who might know what to do about a bullet in the chest...

I fumble with the pocket button—the fabric's already soaked with blood—yank the bandage out... Rishad grabs it from me and puts the pad in place, lays both hands over it and presses down much harder than I possibly could.

Sam's still yelling... "Don't waste ammo! Hold your fire unless you see a target!" ...my subconscious is clinging to his voice, terrified it will suddenly be cut off...

"Isaar!" I shout, over the gunfire, "Isaar, *what do we do?*"

He doesn't seem to hear me, he's too far in shock, but Rishad looks up as though remembering other people exist. His brown skin's almost as grey as Isaar's. Keeping up the pressure on the bandage with one hand, he grabs Isaar's rifle and wriggles the strap free of his brother's body, shoves it at me. "Here, Teresa! This is yours now, okay? Don't put it down!"

Don't put it down 'cause you're going to need it...

I pull the heavy gun to me, two-handed, slip the carry strap over my head with shaking hands. My fingers come away slick with Isaar's blood. Thomas stares at my red hands and loses it completely, wailing full out. What with all the gunfire, it doesn't matter. I wipe my fingers on my jeans and gather him close.

Why am I so terrified for Isaar? Or Sam? What we've tried so hard to avoid has happened at last...

...we've walked right into a bunch of Quabs...

...and now we're all going to die.

35 days earlier...

TERESA

It's the cars I notice first. Actually, it's the *not cars*. Fifteen minutes driving along the main road to Richford during morning rush hour and we've not seen *any* cars.

"Quiet today, isn't it?" I call to Tim.

Tim shrugs and doesn't look back. He's the third driver I've have since I started the job last September, and the most laid back. See if he sticks it out. It's the longest school run, an hour each way out to Thomas's village, and underpaid. But I like the scenery and since I've been at it for almost a year I've got to know the children too well to want to change. April and June have a hospital appointment, though, so it's just Thomas this morning.

"Air fee..." says Thomas, trying to regain my attention.

"Air field," I enunciate clearly. "Did you go to the airfield at the weekend and watch the planes?"

"Yeh," beams Thomas.

"Bet that was fun." Half my mind is on the empty road. I look out the back window but there really isn't any traffic fuming behind the minibus. Not normal. "I'm wondering if the road is closed ahead," I tell Tim. "Everyone else may have heard it on the radio."

Our radio hasn't worked since someone disconnected it from the battery or something two weeks after I started and wiped its memory—no one can find the code to unlock it again.

Another shrug from Tim.

Thomas starts to unscrew his water bottle lid. Attention seeking again, but...

"You know you'll be wet the rest of the way to school if you do that."

Thomas grins and takes the lid off. I take bottle and lid away from him and tuck the refastened bottle down the side of the seat, ignoring his pout. Despite his limited vocabulary and almost non-existent sense of danger, in many ways Thomas is

166

pretty much like any other seven-year-old, naughty included.

"How's your stepfather treating you now, then, Teresa?" calls Tim.

I sigh, but manage not to roll my eyes. "He's my *father*, and it's the same as usual. He must see it's too late for me to go back to school and do his precious Science A levels, but he doesn't let on."

"Still doesn't like you being on the bus, then?"

"I think the busking bothers him more."

Tim shakes his head to himself. "Don't know when you find time to study for that A level of yours."

"It's only one subject. It's not so hard to fit in." I'm teaching myself for the one exam I actually want to sit, with a few private lessons out of my wages.

"You've got a license and everything for the busking, right? Why's it bother him so much?"

"Who knows. Everyone else who left school after GCSE is on the dole, would he rather that?" I don't really want to slag my Dad off to someone I've only known for three weeks, so I give Thomas my attention again—eagerly received. I still have half an eye on the road. No cars. Definitely closed. We might as well turn around now and go round by the side roads. But Tim clearly isn't going to bother unless he has to.

"Wha time?" asks Thomas.

"Five minutes to nine."

He doesn't understand time yet, but he can tell there's something in it he hasn't quite figured out, so he keeps asking. Richford is over the next row of hills—quarter of an hour to Richford Special School, unless we have to make a long diversion, which is looking increasingly likely.

Thomas prattles cheerfully in his growing vocabulary; I answer the familiar questions rather absent-mindedly and keep an eye on the empty road. But as we approach the hills... I lean forward and stare out of the windscreen. "Tim... what do you make of that?"

Pillars of smoke rise into the air on the skyline, five... six... at least seven of them. The fires must be scattered over the whole of Richford!

"Weird," admits Tim. "It's hardly bonfire night."

July, it isn't even close.

"Resa?" Thomas has his unhappy face on. Sensing the uneasiness that's curling in my gut.

"Lot of gardeners burning their rubbish," I say cheerfully, and try to feel calm and unconcerned, 'cause Thomas won't be fooled by just words.

As we drive on, another pillar of smoke begins to rise, quickly join by another. And another. What can be causing them? Why does our radio have to be broken? Something pretty bad must be happening to cause that much smoke. An innocent accident? The best-case scenario?

"Tim, d'you think we should find a farm house and see if they know what's happened in Richford?"

"You can't call the office?"

"I left my phone on charge."

Tim doesn't do mobiles. One of the first things he told me, with great pride.

"Well, we'll be able to see the town from the top of the hills, we might as well carry on."

"Are you..." My voice squeaks slightly and I have to clear my throat. "Are you sure it's a good idea to get closer?"

"Why not? It must be a problem with the gas mains, or kids letting off smoke bombs, or a load of road traffic accidents. Or some big coincidence of all three. Can't be anything very wrong."

Why can't there be? Bad things happen. I've known that since Mum...

Thomas is getting wide-eyed again.

"Here, Thomas, do you want some more water? Don't take the lid off, though..."

Gas mains, huh? For that many to catch fire, there'd have to be a big earthquake or something. And what are the odds, here in the UK? *And* we'd have noticed. I eye the smoke. Going on too long to be smoke bombs, surely? And traffic accidents? How many accidents result in fire, let alone...? I try to count the smoke columns but can no longer do it. Too many. Smoke everywhere. Can there be... rioting? Why on earth? Things are picking up, and Richford is doing better than most. But what does that leave? There's a word I really don't want to think.

Terrorism.

Since the kidnapping of those poor schoolgirls last summer, there's been one attack after another. But all that smoke... it would have to be on a huge scale. "Tim, I think we should stop and find out what's going on."

"Relax, Teresa. Don't go paranoid on me."

"It's not paranoid to think this is very strange. We haven't seen any other cars for half an hour, do you realize. Half an hour! And half of Richford is on fire or something. There is something really, really wrong, and you just want us to go driving into it like idiots!"

"Calm down, girl. You're overreacting. We'll be late if we stop."

"Better safe than sorry."

"We'll see what's up from the brow of the hills, okay?"

I grit my teeth together. Is he totally stupid! *Something* is happening. I feel cold right down to the core of stomach. I'm not very good at remembering to chat to God throughout the day, but I speak to Him now. *Please don't let something be happening, Lord, please?* But it already is. Smoke is rising from our side of the hill, now. From further up the road we're on.

"Ah, see, there's a car coming," says Tim. "Told you you're panicking."

"Try and stop them and find out..."

But the small red car comes tearing up the road at an extraordinary speed. Tim winds down the window and waves half-heartedly, but the car simply roars past, flashing its lights wildly—hazards, main beams and all—leaving nothing but the smell of overstressed engine and the memory of the row of small, neat round holes across its bonnet and side.

"Huh, he's in a hurry," says Tim.

"Didn't you see the bullet holes?"

He swears. "That's what they were! There must be

169

something up!"

Sounds properly spooked. *Finally!*

"So come on, let's find a farm quick and stop. Or better, turn around and follow that car!"

"What? No way, I've got to get back to Richford."

"You can't just drive Thomas and I into the middle of whatever is happening up ahead!"

"My family are in Richford! They're more important than some retard!"

"What?" I gasp. For a moment I choke in rage. "You don't know what's happening! How can you help your family if you get killed! We need to get away from here and get some *facts!*"

"I've gotta get back!"

The maniac is actually accelerating towards whatever has caused that closest plume of smoke. For a moment terror and helplessness make my head ring.

"STOP THE BUS!" I scream with every scrap of volume and authority I can muster. "STOP THE BUS RIGHT NOW, I'M GETTING OFF!"

SAM

The sound of a distant explosion draws me from sleep. Muffled gunfire. *Argh, Rish, Isaar, what sort of time is this to be watching a noisy war film? Some of us were writing essays until late last night, you know.* Should I bang on the floor, get them to turn it down a bit? But I'm sinking back into sleep again already...

"*Sam!*" Footsteps pound up the stairs. "*Sam!*" Isaar bursts in, yelling my name, his brown skin unusually pale. "Get up, quickly!"

At the look on his face I lurch upright in bed, my mind racing. Has someone got Rish? Extremists? Far-right thugs? I reach for the cricket bat I've kept beside my bed ever since Rish and Isaar tweeted photos of themselves in their army uniform last summer and stagger to my feet. "Is it Rish? Where is he?"

"He's fine, but we've got to *go*. Get dressed, *quickly!* Bring the bat!" Isaar dashes back out again; I hear him leaping down the stairs.

Go? Go *where?* I've never seen Isaar scared before, not even when we got surrounded by that bunch of racist louts one night. But he's scared now. Really scared.

Then I realize that those gunshots and explosions aren't coming from downstairs. They're coming from somewhere outside.

I dress. Quickly.

TERESA

Tim slams the brakes on and brings us to a halt with a nasty jolt. "Fine, get out!"

"Wha? Wha, Resa?" sobs Thomas, his face scrunching up with imminent meltdown.

"Hush, Thomas..." I slip off my seatbelt and fling back the sliding door. Yanking the restraining straps from Thomas's folded wheelchair, I chuck it out onto the grass of the verge.

"What the hell are you doing?"

"You've made it perfectly clear you don't consider Thomas your responsibility, but I consider him to be mine, so he's staying with me."

"Good! Just hurry up!"

Thomas begins to cry full out. I kick his pack lunch and school bag off the bus, grab his soft cloth helmet and stick it on his head—don't stop to fasten it 'cause Tim is revving the engine and inching forwards. Thomas is far too big now, but I take off his seatbelt and for once lift him bodily down out of the bus. Tim barely waits for me to free one hand and slam the door before he's tearing off down the road.

The *maniac!*

I ease Thomas to the ground with a gasp. "You really are too big to lift, now, mate."

He carries on crying. I fasten his hat and look around. We're standing by the edge of a field ditch—no hedges for several hundred meters. It feels horribly exposed. A small wood comes up to the road back the way we've come. I unfold the

171

wheelchair quickly and manoeuvre Thomas into it—he can walk and even run now, but his balance is still iffy. I want to stop and comfort him but... time enough for that when we're off the road.

Gathering up schoolbag and packed lunch, I start pushing. No smoke in this direction. Birds sing. Still no cars but... as my heart rate steadies I can't help wondering. What if Tim was right the first time? And there isn't anything wrong? Perhaps they weren't really holes, perhaps they were bullet hole stickers. Just a boy racer flashing his lights and showing off.

A look over my shoulder at the smoke and I go on pushing as fast as I can. Okay, I may be going to have an awfully red face if I've got it wrong—in fact, I'm going to be in a lot of trouble—would this count as kidnapping?—*but*. That's a lot of smoke. And since when are boy racers out at this time in the morning?

"It's all right, Thomas," I tell him, as we go. "It's all right. Tim has to go and check something in Richford, so we're going to do some Forest School today until he comes back for us. You like Forest School, don't you? It's fun. Perhaps we'll visit a farm. And have a picnic. How about that?"

His howls die down, but his sniffs don't. There are a lot of intellectual things he doesn't get, but he isn't stupid. He's never ever been taken off the bus anywhere other than school, let alone with two adults terrified and screaming at each other. He knows things are Not Right.

I need my breath for pushing as the road heads up an incline. Reach the trees, reassurance afterwards.

Then what?

JOHN
"Come *on*," calls Mama from the door. "You'll be late for school."

I grab my pencil case from the lounge table and hurry along the hall. James is holding my rucksack—I take it from him as we go out onto the step and put my pencil case inside as Mama locks the door.

"And then," as we skip down the steps James launches back into what he was saying when I rushed back into the lounge, "the dinosaur put its head right into the car and it was going to eat us up, but I yelled, 'Lord Jesus, help!' and slipped my rosary over its muzzle and it simply couldn't get its mouth open! So it ran off, roaring and thrashing its tail. And I woke up. And I was really glad it was a dream, because otherwise I'd have lost my rosary."

"Never mind the dinosaurs roaming around eating people," says Mama, smiling as she hurries us along. She overslept, so we'll be late if we're not careful.

"That would've been bad too," James agrees.

"I don't know; your imagination." Mama shakes her head, but she's still smiling.

"He didn't make it up, he *dreamt* it," I point out. "So strictly speaking..." A loud bang from somewhere towards the city centre distracts me. "What are they doing, Mama? That's the third one in ten minutes."

Mama frowns. "I'm honestly not sure, John. I suppose it must be building work."

A chattering, rattling series of retorts has now started.

"Is that a pneu... pneu...matic drill?" says James, pronouncing the word carefully.

Mama listens, still frowning. "Probably. Or something like that. Sounds a bit different. Oh well, come on..."

JAMES

"*I* dreamt our Dada came back," John says, as we carry on. Then adds quickly, as Mama's face closes, "But that's not going to happen, I know."

"But it *might,*" I object. "What Mama *said* was that the only way he'd come back would be if he found Jesus." I remember her words exactly. "He could find Jesus, couldn't he, Mama?"

Mama... winces? "Oh, James, anything is possible with God, but when I said that I meant that it was as near impossible

173

as makes no difference. You know your father's Muslim, and he's really *not* a tolerant man."

"And he left because of you finding Jesus," says John. "Right before we were born. We know. But *why* can't he find Jesus too?"

"Marvellous as it would be, it's not likely to happen," says Mama firmly. "And no talking about any of it to anyone..."

"We know, we know." John rolls his eyes. "He mustn't find out where we are."

"Unless he finds Jesus?" I can't help asking.

"James," Mama strokes my hair gently. "I know you want a father. But you *don't* want your real one. Please trust me on this."

I sigh. I've had the impression Mama thinks our father is bad news before, but this is the clearest she's been about it.

We head on along the road in silence.

JOHN

"It's really busy this morning," I say, as a whole family rush from a nearby house, leap into the car and drive off at a positively reckless speed. "Did the *whole city* oversleep this morning? Everyone's in such a hurry."

Mama takes hold of each of our hands, though we're old enough to walk beside her on our own now, and marches on. I can see her looking from side to side, though, watching the unusual activity. We didn't have the TV on this morning; perhaps there was something on the news. I shoot a look at James. His brow wrinkles slightly as he looks back at me. Mama's silence is making him nervous too.

We come out onto the main road, and for a moment we just stare in shock. The traffic is nose to tail, stationary. Cars are honking and revving and inching forward. As we watch, a car actually rams up against the car in front, wheels spinning against the tarmac as it tries to force it forwards. There are people on foot, as well, hurrying, running, some are carrying bags, bulging bin liners... there's a little girl about our age carrying a hamster cage. All going in the same direction. Away from the city centre.

"Oh Lord, what's happening?" Mama whispers, then raises her voice and catches a woman's arm. "Excuse me, what's happening?"

The woman won't stop. She pulls free. "They're coming!" she calls over her shoulder, face contorted in fear. "We've got to get out!"

Mama hesitates for a moment, a look of unusual indecision on her face.

"Should we go with all the people, Mama?" I ask, annoyed to find a sob trying to get into my voice. "Or should we go home?"

But it's too late. Another wave of people surges along the road, pushing all around us, carrying us with them. I hang on to Mama's hand. There are more bangs in the distance. The pneumatic drill keeps on going, in short bursts. I can hear duller retorts now, like... firecrackers.

Or... gunshots?

I gasp and cling more tightly to Mama's hand in the press of people. "Mama? Mama, are those *gunshots?*" I've only ever heard them on TV.

Mama looks ever so pale, now. She grabs another person's shoulder. "*Who's* coming?" she demands.

The man glances at Mama's ebony hair and beautiful brown skin that she got from her parents who were born somewhere a long way away called Pakistan.

"*Your lot!*" he snaps. "*Your lot* are coming!"

TERESA

The sun is shining and the Oxfordshire countryside is beautiful. So peaceful without the cars. If not for that lack, we could just be out for a walk.

Rat-tat-tat-tat-tat. Rat-tat-tat-tat-tat.

A vicious chattering sound breaks the silence from somewhere behind us, further down the road. I spin around and stare, heart pounding. I can see nothing. Another burst of what

175

has to be some kind of automatic gunfire and the sound of an impact. Then nothing...

Two shots in quick succession. How can I be sure they're shots?

I am, though. I spin around and begin pushing again, breaking into a run. Still several hundred meters to the trees...

"You're too heavy!" I pant, as Thomas begins to sob again. The sound of an engine revving comes from behind us. I shut up and push. I push so fast Thomas actually begins to giggle between sobs.

"Fly-eeng, fly-eeng!"

Lord, don't let me tip him out at this speed!

The vehicle is coming closer. All that open road... How close will they need to be to see us? I run and run.

There are the woods, almost there, almost. Here... I shove the chair across a shallow section of ditch and plough on into the trees. The loose soil and leaves should be impossible to push through; I must be running on pure adrenalin.

The engine is so close. I stop behind a reasonably bushy tree and unsnap Thomas's buckle, bundle him out, fold the chair and drop it on its side, then press Thomas to the ground.

"Lie down, okay, lie down... Lie still. Don't make a sound." I put my finger to my lips for emphasis and make sure I have an arm around him in case he does try to get up. He still sniffs a little, but I am so frightened it clearly leaves him too scared to howl.

I angle my head so I can see the road. If it's a civilian vehicle, I'll run out and try to get us a lift out of here...

It *is* a civilian vehicle. But I feel no desire to run out. Or even twitch a muscle. It's a pickup truck, loaded with foreign-looking men without uniform, all swathed in headscarves, yelling and brandishing rifles in a very un-British-army-like manner. It could've just driven out of a news bulletin. Surely it belongs in a desert somewhere?

I clutch Thomas and I lie very, very still.

JASPER

"Come on, Molly, over here," I call.

My black and white pony lifts her head and snorts at me, but deigns to amble along the hedgerow to where I'm standing clutching an armful of tasty summer foliage. She snatches a quick mouthful as I step up to her withers baskets and tip the stuff in.

"Greedy guts," I say, taking a bunch of rabbits from a nearby tree branch and tossing them across her neck. I just need to get Edith back, now, and collect my nets. But right now, there's someone creeping along behind the hedge... Trying to, anyway.

Molly snorts at me again—then blows out a huge breath, nostrils flaring.

"I know, William's aftershave's pretty pongy, isn't it?"

"I don't know how you do it, boy," says the old farmer, looking over the hedge. "I'll never sneak up on you, will I?"

"I should hope not," I agree. "Not unless I've got a stinking cold, anyway, and even then, you make so much noise when you walk."

"You certainly know how to boost a fellow's confidence."

I grin and he smiles back. Actually, seeing William doesn't make me feel entirely happy. We haven't been here since last summer—we came a little earlier in the season last year. And I remember the video he showed me, of those kidnapped schoolgirls. And how seeing it brought it all back, about how I helped search for them—and found them. Two of them. Tied up in that horsebox... I shake my head to drive the memory away. Fortunately William is making a fuss of Molly and doesn't see.

"Anyway," he says, "I've just been down to remind your dad not to do any of his *hocus pocus* while he's here."

"He won't."

"Will *you?*"

"I don't believe in that New Age stuff."

"Since when?"

"Since I made the mistake of reading up about it. It's so

obviously been made up in, like, the last hundred years! *Um*... don't tell Dad I said that, though."

"You'll have to 'fess up sooner or later, lad."

"Yeah, but I reckon it'll wait till I know what I *do* believe. I was quite happy thinking of his little gods and goddesses as forces of nature but now here's Gran saying they're fallen angels—and *that* might account for the problems you've had. You know Gran's travelling with us now, right?"

"Yes, I met her when I was down at the caravan—caravans, now. I thought there was a family rift?"

"Well, having accepted she can't manage by herself any more, she preferred the idea of travelling with Mum—and I reckon Dad, too, 'cause he treats her right—rather than any of my uncles and aunts. So she's overlooking the whole 'eloping with a long-haired pagan hippie' thing. Though, that's ancient history now, surely."

William unsuccessfully hides a smile. "For *you*, boy. Anyway, I figured you'd be up here thinning out my rabbits for me."

"Have you shot *any* since we were last here? The place is hopping."

William smiles sheepishly. "Been busy, lad."

"Thought you were retired."

"Well..." He shrugs dismissively, then glances around as a rabbit bolts from its hole into one of my nets—I move that way but he forestalls me. "I've got it, I've got it..."

He straightens after only a moment and holds up the straggler. "Can you spare this one?"

"'Course. It's your rabbit."

"Won't Margery be impressed by me bringing this home when I didn't so much as take a shotgun out with me!"

"Sorry, Mum's been up to the farmhouse already. Margery knows we're here."

"Ah well. She makes a mean rabbit stew."

"Umm, I've had it."

"Of course you have. Well, help yourself, as usual. But do bring me a nice hare sometime. And a brace of pheasants.

Margery's very partial to a brace of pheasants, as you know."

"Misplaced your shotgun, have you?" I tease him.

"Hah. That's no joking matter, the way things are, boy. I keep it locked up when not in use, and so should anyone with any sense. Lots of weapons been stolen, lately."

"Oh." I tried very hard to listen to the news a bit more, after what happened last year, but it was just too depressing. I've almost given up on it again. "Well, we don't have any firearms, so no one will bother us."

"True. Well, I'll leave you to it."

RISHAD

Sam hurtles down the stairs and into the living room, trying to do up his shirt with the cricket bat tucked under his arm. "What the hell is happening?"

"Unconfirmed reports," says the newscaster on the TV, "suggest that unidentified militants are attempting to seize control of areas of Oxford and Bristol..."

"Unconfirmed, huh?" I snap at her, just as the screen goes fuzzy and the picture disappears entirely. "Well, looks like *unconfirmed* has just taken out your transmitter!" Then what I just heard sinks in...

"Bristol..." mutters Isaar, horror in his eyes.

I pull out my phone to call Mum and Dad and warn them—but I've got no signal. Have the militants taken out the mobile transmitters as well? I pick up the landline... silence from the handset. "Damn it!"

"There's nothing we can do," says Isaar softly, pocketing his own useless phone. "We have to look after ourselves."

He's right, of course. But the thought of Mum and Dad and our little sisters caught up in something like this...

"What's going on?" asks Sam again, though from his tone he knows what's going on now and is hoping against hope someone will say it's not true.

"Terrorists are overrunning the city. Look out the window."

Sam does so. Cautiously. But there are no terrorists in sight yet, just fleeing Oxonians. Pillars of smoke are clearly visible, though, and a sudden, closer explosion cracks one pane of glass.

"Come *on!*" I say. "We've got to get out!"

Isaar has his head by the radio, now, listening. "Apparently the government are saying... oh, this has gone dead now as well... but the government are telling people to stay in their homes."

"To hell with that," I say.

"I don't know," says Sam. "If these people are on a killing spree, then running outside where they can shoot you isn't necessarily a good idea."

"I think it's worse than that, Sam," says Isaar quietly. "I don't think this is just the latest terrorist atrocity. I think this is a takeover bid."

"Which makes staying put a *very bad idea*," I say. "So come *on*, let's go!"

"Right, let's grab the knives from the kitchen," says Sam decisively, "and get out."

He's convinced. Good. Because I'd hate to go without him, but I'm not sticking around here with Isaar for anything. I'd be prepared to go along with the lunatics, so long as it was only words, to save us, but I know my twin. He won't knuckle under to these people. And they'll kill him for it.

Of course, if they find out we're in the army, even merely the University Officer Training Corps, they'll kill us both anyway...

SAM

Rish grabs a cereal box, chucks the bag of cereal onto the work top, and unfolds the box into one large piece of cardboard. "Get some parcel tape," he says.

When he starts tearing the cardboard into three pieces, I get it. He's making knife sheaths. I dash back into the lounge and find some tape in a cupboard, bring it back. It's no good if we cut ourselves on our own weapons, after all.

Weapons... Rish has already folded the cardboard around the three sharpest knives he can find, and immediately starts wrapping tape around them.

Why is the word 'weapons' niggling at me?

Oh no... I dash back to the lounge again and look out the window, trying to judge from the smoke how much of the city has fallen. There are several hundred rifles in the magazine building. Has it been overrun, yet? The chances the army got them out seem slim. The attack seems to have come out of nowhere. If the terrorists get those weapons...

Not that they seem short of guns, from all the firing... I can feel my mind seeking reasons—excuses—as to why I shouldn't worry too much about it. But hundreds of rifles... how can that not be a huge help to them? How many people could they kill, just with those...

I pull out my phone, to try to phone HQ and see if they know what's happening at the magazine... No signal. Of course.

You don't even know if the magazine is still reachable, Sam... But right now, I can't just be Sam, can I? I have to be Second Lieutenant Worthing. And Second Lieutenant Worthing has a duty to get the hell down to the magazine and try to stop those weapons falling into the wrong hands.

If I do this, I could be dead within the next hour. I swallow hard. I can feel sweat on my forehead. I never thought I'd hesitate in a situation like this. But I can see now that I've actually never had to be brave before. Not really. Because I've never been truly afraid.

I swallow again, and dash back into the kitchen. "Change of plan, Rish," I say. "You take Isaar and get out of here. I'll be right behind you, I hope, but I've got to go somewhere first."

Rish looks startled, then I see the same Awful Realization in his eyes. "You're going to the magazine."

"What else can I do? I don't think they're there yet. There's still a chance."

Rish glances at Isaar—I see the anguished indecision on his face.

"What about the magazine?" asks Isaar.

"There are a couple of hundred rifles there," says Rish quietly. "The terrorists will think *Eid* has come early."

"I didn't think of that. We have to go with Sam and help."

Rish actually closes his eyes for a moment. The struggle between his sense of duty and his most basic instinct—protect his gentle brother—is plain on his face.

"Rish!" says Isaar more firmly. "We're going with Sam!"

"Fine," says Rish grimly, shoving one of the sheathed knives into Isaar's hands. "You'd better take this, then."

ISAAR

I look at the kitchen knife lying in my hands in its makeshift sheathe, and try to imagine actually stabbing someone with it. I'm just not sure I could. I mean, just possibly, if they were actually hurting someone. But I still can't picture it. I'm a third year medical student, for pity's sake. I just want to *heal* people...

Rish hands another knife to Sam, and Sam tries sticking it through his belt, but it looks like it's going to fall out. He shove it in his pocket instead... but that's obviously not going to work either.

Rish has just lifted his trouser leg and shoved the knife down his boot. I stuck my tall army boots on as well, and so did Sam, so we do the same.

"Let's go, if we're going," says Rish, heading towards the front door. "I do wish I could call Mr Asmani. Tell him to just take the car and go..."

Because of the university's ban on student cars in the city centre, we keep our car out in the suburbs on the drive of an old gentleman from the mosque, who no longer drives but likes having a car parked outside as a burglar deterrent.

"Everything's down," says Sam, snatching his OTC beret from the hall table and pocketing it. He glances at the bat and shakes his head slightly. Impractical. "Transmitters, power..."

We open the door and look out at the chaos outside. Cars and pedestrians, pouring along. Well, the pedestrians are pouring along, the cars are stationary.

"We are never going to manage to get through that!" says Rish.

No, we'll be going against the flow...

"If we can get along just far enough, we can get down onto the tow path. That might not be so busy," says Sam. "We'd better take the bikes, there's no time to lose."

We unchain the bicycles quickly and begin to force our way through the crush. The cars are literally bumper to bumper—we have to climb across the bonnets to get to the other side of the road. Rish takes point, determinedly forging his way through the crush, and Sam and I keep close behind him. Soon we reach the track that goes down to the river, and are able to get on our bikes and ride. The towpath is busy, lots of smarter and more athletic university students jogging towards the city's eastern outskirts, making much better time than everyone up on the main road. But it's not so busy we can't get through, ringing our bells like mad to get people to clear a path.

"You're going the wrong way!" a few people yell. "Turn around!"

We're cycling straight towards people who will kill us if they can. I'd love to turn around. I'd really, really love to. But one thought of those rifles and I know I can't.

"They're on their way to join them!" a man shouts, as we pass him, and I sense the sudden change in the mood.

"Stop them!" shouts someone else. Hands reach for us...

"Don't be stupid!" snaps Sam. "We're soldiers, get out the way!"

Sam has been a fully commissioned officer since completing Sandhurst last summer, although he's still studying at Uni on his army bursary, and the authority in his voice makes itself felt—the reaching hands hesitate. Rish accelerates rapidly, we follow, and the ugly moment is left behind us.

Just *Allah* alone knows how many deranged terrorists up ahead...

TERESA

The truck has roared on its way, the men shouting loud enough to be heard over the engine, though I couldn't make out what they were saying. I've carried right on lying still. *This can't be happening. This cannot be happening.* My whole body is shaking. I can feel the sobs trying to force their way out of my throat. I fight them back with everything I have. Thomas is frightened enough already.

Eventually I manage to sit up and put my back to the tree, so I won't be visible from the road. What was that shooting? I've a horrible idea.

More to the point, what do I do now?

One pickup truck full of guys can't have caused all that smoke, so we must now be right in the middle of a whole bunch of them. *Oh, why wouldn't Tim turn around? We could've been out of here...*

No point thinking about that, though.

I have to visit the site of the shooting. I have to know just how bad things are. What if T... what if someone is there, hurt? By myself I can jog and be there and back very quickly. If I hear an engine I can dive in the ditch and be fairly invisible. Thank God I'm wearing black jeans and a green tunic, no bright colours! Unlike Thomas, who is wearing a yellow t-shirt, worse luck. But what to do about Thomas?

Pushing the wheelchair more easily over the loose ground with Thomas walking beside it, I move to the back of the wood. The trees go further than I've realized, so that gets us a good distance from the road. Picking up a couple of pieces of discarded baler twine as I go, one in the wood and one from the edge of the field we come out on, I knot them around Thomas, harness-fashion. Add reins and tie them to a tree. Move the wheelchair well out of reach, then have a good look to be sure there's nothing else he can climb onto, fall off and strangle himself, should he get the twine around his neck. Nothing. No way to guarantee his silence, but hopefully he'll be too scared to be noisy. He's never left alone normally. Anyway, no one will hear him over an engine, will they?

"Thomas, I've got to go and look at something, I'll be right back. Lots of birds live here, so if you stay very quiet while I'm gone, you should see some of them."

His eyes have gone wide again and he grabs my hand. "No, no, Resa stay here..."

I put my other arm around him and give him a quick half hug, then pry my hand free. "I'm coming back, Thomas, I won't be long. You just keep quiet and watch the birds, okay?"

"Resa! Resa, no! *Resa! Resa!*" His screams make my heart ache as I walk briskly away. He's terrified, poor kid. But if I take him with me, we'll be sitting ducks.

Once I'm out of sight, his cries peter off rapidly and silence falls over the wood. I break into a jog. Perhaps it's foolish to risk going down the road, but I just have to have some information about what is happening, *something* to go on!

Why didn't I remember to charge my phone last night? Why does Tim have to be a technophobe! No use. It's no use thinking that! I have no phone, it's too late.

I make much better time once I reach the road, especially on the downhill stretches. I jog all the way into the town centre every day after the morning school run, with my violin, music and music stand on my back, and back again before the afternoon run, so this is something I can do no problem. I enjoy running. Usually. Just now I listen so hard my head rings, and my heart inches up into my throat at every bend.

I didn't check what time I left the wood, but after about ten or fifteen minutes I see something white up ahead, at the bottom of another gentle incline. The minibus. I stop and look around, then climb over a field gate—it doesn't squeak, thank God!—and follow the road along the other side of the hedge. There's probably no one there, *but*.

The hedge is bushy with summer growth, and once I reach the bottom I have to go to the next field gateway to get a look. The minibus is rammed into the dry stone wall opposite, though from here both look deceptively undamaged. I can't see anyone, and all is silent, save a few birds calling here and there. No sign of Tim, either. Has he been taken away?

I scale the gate and dart across the road. Ease open the passenger door and look in. Bullet holes stitch across the windscreen and driver's side door, which hangs open, and there's blood on the seat. I swallow. Open the glove box and take out the first aid kit. Clutch it to me in futile readiness and quietly closing the door again, go around the back of the bus to the other side.

That's where Tim is.

From the grotesque way he lies, his legs bent under him, he was dragged from the bus and forced to his knees.

Then someone put two bullets through his head.

ALLELUIA

I stow my bag in the overhead locker and settle into my seat. It's always nice once you're actually on the plane, rather than just waiting around at an airport. I've got a window seat, too. I don't usually care when hopping back and forth across the pond for Thanksgiving or whatever, but this way I might see a little bit of Rome as we come in to land.

A middle-aged lady takes the seat beside me, as a roar of engines announces a plane taking off. We exchange a quick, polite smile, then she gets busy on her phone, making the most of the time before she has to put it away.

I turn back to the window. There are a surprising number of planes; somehow I thought Bristol airport would be smaller than this. I would normally have flown from London, where I'm studying, but since I was going to be in Bristol yesterday speaking at a youth event, it made more sense to fly from here. Of course, all the teens really wanted to hear about was the kidnapping last summer, and how I persuaded forty-eight of my schoolmates to escape with me by jumping out of a horsebox on the M4 while doing about fifty miles an hour. But I also made sure to remind them about the two hundred and nineteen girls whose fate remains unknown.

I glance around again someone takes the third seat, but he's not looking my way. Then my gaze falls on the front cover of the in-flight magazine, and something catches painfully in my chest. I take it from the seat pocket and look at it properly. The cover photo is of a girl dressed in school uniform, with mid-length brown hair, a calm smile, and a pair of life-filled brown eyes. 'Ruth Kerril—Schoolgirl on Fast Track to Sainthood' says the caption. I open the magazine and find the article.

Ruth Kerril was fifteen years old when she was kidnapped from Chisbrook School near Newbury, with two hundred and seventy-six of her fellow students. When told she must convert to Islam or be killed, she refused, and she held to her Christian faith throughout the brutal beating that followed, remaining resolute even as her attacker cut her throat.

Faithful Catholics were clamouring for her canonization almost the moment the details of her horrific martyrdom came to light, but Vatican commentators were still surprised when a bare month later, Pope Dominic announced that he had put the process in motion, waiving the five year wait that is normally required. As the Pope admitted in an interview shortly afterwards, "This just isn't the sort of thing I usually do. I am someone who feels that rules are generally there for a good reason."

He went on to describe how Ruth Kerril's story had 'taken root in his soul'. "I'd be trying to pray, and I'd just be thinking about this courageous girl, who showed such faith to the very end, and I felt more and more strongly that her example is one that many countries need *now*. Finally, I said, 'Lord, You can't want me to waive the waiting period, surely?' And once I'd said that, I really could not get it out of my head and I realized that actually, that was exactly what He was asking me to do. So naturally I obeyed."

I read that bit twice. After several years at school with Ruth, hearing her explaining all the weird Catholic things Evangelicals like me tend to get so het up about, I know a lot them aren't really quite so weird—or unbiblical—as I've always been taught. But it's still strange to read about the Pope so clearly following the promptings of the Holy Spirit. It's even stranger to be flying to Rome for my friend's beatification. By the end of tomorrow, over a billion Catholics world-wide will be praying to 'Blessed Ruth'.

I carry on with the article, as another plane opens up its engines for takeoff.

> An even greater cause for astonishment among some is that a team of Sainthood investigators (known to often take years—or even decades—to complete their task) have been able to conclude their examination of the evidence in a mere six months. But as Pope Dominic said, "The tragic fact is that the investigation has been very quick, because her life was so very short. There simply wasn't that much to be examined."

And all very conclusive, no doubt. Ruth was the sort of person everyone would call special, whether they were religious or not. Dad was a little unsure about me attending this beatification thing, I could tell, but he didn't try to stop me. He and Mom are off on Mission again in the Middle East, anyway. But the Catholics took the trouble to invite me—the invitation was from Pope Dominic himself—well, from his secretary. And although the whole 'Blessed' thing doesn't really mean much to me, Ruth did, and this thing tomorrow is basically about a bunch of people publically acknowledging how brave and good she was. So I want to be there.

The cabin stewards are trying to cram the last few suitcases into the overhead lockers. It's July, no surprise the flight is packed. Another roar of airplane engines—so much for three minute intervals! I've never heard so many big planes take off so close together! I'm about to turn back to the article again when our engines start. I wouldn't pay it any heed, only the cabin crew look startled. Actually, they don't usually start the engines until the cabin stewards are sitting down, do they?

When the plane lurches forward, making a case fall out onto someone's head, and begins to taxi across the tarmac, the cabin steward leaves the case where it's fallen and practically runs up the aisle to bang on the cockpit door. "Captain? Captain, why are we moving? Captain?"

There's no reply.

My body suddenly feels ice cold all over. What's happening?

No, Lord, please. Please, not again. Not again. Not again...

TERESA

I'm down on my knees, my head spinning. My stomach heaves. My head is white and buzzy with terror.

They didn't just fire on the bus to stop it. They dragged poor bullet-ridden Tim out and just... just shot him, for no reason.

I throw up again.

I was furious with Tim for abandoning us, but... didn't wish *this* on him.

More vomit. My every dizzy thought seems to prompt another spasm.

Finally my stomach is empty and the dry heaves die away. What to do? Thomas is back there on his own, I have to hurry up. Surely the army will deal with this pretty quickly? We just have to make sure those lunatics don't catch us before they do. If we lie low until tomorrow, it'll probably all be over. Because I won't get far on foot, not with Thomas.

Or... I eye the minibus. I know how to drive... in theory. I've never done it. Only thing is, those men are ahead of us now. But we can go down back roads... In a big white minibus, visible for miles? Look what happened to Tim. The time to drive out of this was probably back when that red car passed us. Still...

I go back round to the blood-free passenger side, climb in and lean across to turn the key. Nothing. Absolutely nothing. The wall has won this one. So that's that.

Searching the minibus quickly, I take the bag of winter emergency supplies from the overhead locker—three foil blankets and three bars of chocolate—add the daily vehicle check notebook and pen, and take it out to where I left the first aid kit. Steeling myself, I approach Tim's body. I know what I want, but I'm not sure if I can... *You have to, Teresa, just do it...* Oeuw...

He's half-lying on the pocket I need to get to. Gingerly I take hold of his shirt and ease him over. That gives too good a look at his gore-drenched body and... what's left of his face, slack and empty. I shove my hand into his pocket, yank out his penknife pride and joy and bolt. Manage to get several feet away before the heaving grips me again. *Clearly I'm not cut out to be a grave-robber.* My brain's attempt at humour just makes me throw up yet again, painfully.

When the spasm's passed I wipe the knife on the grass a few times and pocket it. Hopefully Tim won't mind me borrowing it. I'll return it to his family after this is over, if... if they're okay. What have those men done in Richford? Are Dad and Cheryl and little Mikey all right? I try to push the thoughts away—but sobs force their way out of my throat and for long moments I can do nothing but kneel there, shaking, as they tear their way out of me, on and on.

If this is what it is to be scared, then I've never been scared before, never. I've just thought I've been.

Crack. Crack. Crack.

Three sharp retorts from somewhere in the distance finally choke off the tears. I look up, my heart now trying to escape from my mouth instead.

Silence.

All the same... that's too far to the left to be the men that passed us, surely? How many are there? I have to get back to Thomas.

I pick up the meagre bag of supplies, turn to go... hesitate. Go back to Tim and kneel down, not looking at him. I want to cover him in some way, but if the men come back they'll know someone's been here. A half-remembered prayer floats around in my mind, so I whisper that.

"May Tim's soul and the souls of all the faithful depart rest in peace, Amen."

It will have to do. I get up and start running back along the road.

ALLELUIA

Another cabin steward has joined the first one.

"Captain!" they shout, pounding on the door. "Let us in!" The bellow of engines almost drowns them out as another plane on the main runway roars into the sky.

"Cabin crew, seats for takeoff." The clipped words come over the intercom, as though the captain's attention is very much elsewhere.

The cabin staff exchange bewildered looks. We're heading out towards the runway, now, taxiing at unusual speed—and so are all the other planes. I realize that now I look out of the window again. Every aircraft in sight is converging on the main runway at what certainly looks like dangerous speed. Even as I watch, two full size airliners clip wings, skid in two different directions, and roll to a halt, blocking that tarmac. A queue of planes, large and small, grinds to a halt behind them, except for a tiny private plane that literally darts under the two wings and heads straight on onto the runway.

The bellow of plane engines announces another takeoff. So soon? And another plane is already turning out into position. It's like every plane at the airport has suddenly decided they want to take off at the same time.

"Captain, what's going on?" yell the cabin crew.

191

"*Sit down!*" snaps the intercom.

There's a click as though a switch has been pressed, and another voice comes on, hoarse and frantic. "All aircraft, repeat, all aircraft, take off now. Repeat, *take off now*. Do not wait for signals from air traffic control. Repeat, all aircraft, *take off now...*" There's a crash in the background, a couple of sharp retorts and cut off screams. The voice rises, fear and urgency overflowing through the speakers, "*Take off now! Take off now! Take off n...*" Another, louder retort, and the voice cuts off. A thud and a lot of static.

Engines roar as the next plane goes up.

My heart is hammering so hard I think I'm going to throw up. One of the damaged planes is turning out onto the grass, as though trying to clear the slipway, the second... the second, with a bit of metal hanging off its wing, is actually straightening and moving forward again, as though it plans to attempt to takeoff anyway.

Our plane is moving faster, taxiing so quickly we can feel the tail lifting slightly. I peer through the window, trying to see how many planes are ahead of us on our slipway. Two or three. One is waiting to turn onto the main runway. Engines bellow again; a plane from another slipway is already taking off. Then another one... They must be taking off almost nose to tail. After hearing what's happening at air traffic control, I'm glad, rather than worried...

The cabin crew have dived into their seats and are fumbling with their seat belts.

Another plane takes off... But there are still so many. How long before it's our turn?

The plane at the front of our line has spotted a gap, it's moving again, turning out onto the runway.

A streak of smoke and movement through the air... and the turning plane explodes, instantly engulfed in flames. Something slams into our plane, and it swerves sickeningly.

Oh Lord, are the pilots hit?

SAM

The shooting and the explosions are getting so close. Are we even going to make it to the magazine? Part of me rather hopes it's too late. If the building's been overrun, we can turn around and get back across the city and away.

But we jump our bikes down one final set of steps and we're there. Smoke is rising from what looks to be very close by, but no terrorists are in sight. We dump the bikes behind the wall and hurry to the little window by the door...

"Stop!" I hiss, holding up a hand and moving to the side as I realize the window's already been smashed. Rish and Isaar move with me, and we try to approach silently, but some of the glass has fallen outwards and our feet go *crunch-crunch*. No reaction from inside the magazine building, though. Right... nothing for it then. "Is there someone in there?" I call. Not too loud. Even if there isn't one inside, who knows how close the terrorists are?

"I've got a grenade!" comes a strained voice from within. "Clear off or I'll throw it!"

That upper class voice... "And exactly where did you get a grenade, Henry Wrexham?" I retort.

"Sam? Is that you?"

"Yes, it's me, and Rish and Isaar with me."

"Oh, thank God! I thought you were bad guys!"

"We're coming in." I climb quickly through the broken window and head along the building's one and only passage. Henry Wrexham is looking around the corner at the end, pale-faced, and the doors of the two magazines are still closed.

"Where's this phantom grenade, then?" asks Rish.

"Well, of course I don't actually have one," says Henry, in his cultured voice.

"So why did you claim you did? The bad guys would just have chucked an actual grenade straight in here."

If anything, Henry goes even paler. "Didn't think of that," he mutters. "Well, have you got the key, then, Sam?"

My heart drops into my boots. How stupid am *I*? Rushing here like this. Of course I don't have a key. And without one... I turn to look at the great steel magazine doors. Without one, I don't fancy our chances.

"Sam doesn't have a key," says Isaar quietly.

"Then why are you here?"

"Why are *you* here?" I say.

"I came to try and get the rifles away. But I can't get in. It didn't occur to me until I got here."

"Same," I say grimly.

"Oh..."

ALLELUIA

The plane is bumping and rumbling... there's grass outside, we've left the slipway, but we're swinging around, coming parallel to the runway, not quite like we're out of control...

The engines bellow, suddenly, and the acceleration smacks my head back into the head rest like I've never felt it before. My head is stuck sideways, can't straighten it, and I can still see out the window... the plane is shaking like mad, grass is flashing by below, and... there on the main runway, a plane is tearing along. We're racing, wingtip to wingtip, them on the tarmac, us on the grass...

O Lord, aren't there lights and all sorts of things on the grass beside runways? We'll hit something, surely! The plane is rattling, juddering, from the acceleration or from the rough surface under its wheels I can't say.

Judder, judder, judder, judder...

People are screaming. People are shouting, "What's happening! *What's happening?*"

Judder, judder, judder, jud...

Stillness.

Just like that, we're airborne.

As we climb steeply, engines still roaring—no doubt trying to get out of range of any more RPGs, or whatever it was hit that plane—it slowly sinks in. The pilot took off *on the grass!* And thank God he did!

I crane, trying to see the airport, trying to see if other

194

planes are managing to get past the burning one and get off—
trying to see if there are any tiny figures, pointing anything our
way—but all I can see are clouds of black smoke, rising into the
sky.

Every muscle in my body is clenched tight, waiting for that
impact, that ball of flame... I make a big effort to breathe.

Lord, be with us... Lord, get us away...

RISHAD
Crunch-crunch.

We freeze at the sound from outside, then tiptoe around
the corner with undignified haste and freeze again.

"Hello?" quavers a voice from the window.

"Identify yourselves," Sam snaps. Because it sounded like
more than one set of feet.

"Uh... you first..."

"It sounds like Will Herring," says Henry.

"Officer Cadet Herring?" Sam calls.

"Uh... yeah?"

"It's Second Lieutenant Worthing. Who's with you?"

"Uh... Officer Cadet Pollock."

"*Rob?*" says Henry disbelievingly. "Weasel Rob?"

"Apparently," I mutter.

Sam raises his voice. "Okay, you can come inside." The
two of them climb in. It is indeed Rob, as greasy-haired and sly-
eyed as usual. "What are you doing here, you two?" asks Sam.

"Came to save the rifles," says Will.

"Er... yeah. To save them," says Rob.

In other words, Rob came because he wanted a weapon
and Will... probably a bit of both, knowing Will.

"Pollock," says Sam, "you get back by that window and
keep watch. The rest of us need to figure out how to open the
magazines."

"Don't you have a key?" demands Rob.

"No."

Their faces both fall.

"*Window,* Pollock, you're on sentry duty," Sam says grimly, "Now, we're all Oxford university students, finest minds in the country and all that, surely we can figure something out."

"My degree is in Egyptology, not safe breaking," points out Will.

I ignore him; so does Sam. I know we're grasping at straws, but Sam's right, we have to at least *try* to think of a way to get in before we give up and scarper, much as I'm sure we'd all love to skip straight to that.

"Two keys for each magazine," Isaar is muttering. "And then the code. And we've got none of it. Sam, I really don't think we can do it."

I can't think of anything to say to gainsay him; apparently neither can Sam, because he says, "Let's check the store."

The store around the corner is full of sleeping bags, uniform, and totally non-explosive items like that. We search every rack quickly, then give up in disgust and go back to the passage.

"Er, Sam? The shooting's getting closer," calls Rob Pollock nervously. I'm slightly surprised he hasn't sneaked off yet.

Sam hurries back to the window to listen, and I follow. *Blast.* Rob's right. We can't get the rifles out, and unarmed as we are, it's not like we can try to defend the building. It would be suicide in any case, and gain nothing. We'll have to leave.

Sam's just turning, no doubt to give orders to this effect, when we hear an engine approaching. We crouch down quickly. The vehicle stops right outside. *Oh no...* my heart is pounding so hard... cautiously I peep over the window sill... Immediately duck down again.

There's a four-ton military truck outside. We've left it too late...

YESTERDAY & TOMORROW: 1

TOMORROW'S DEAD

COMING SOON

To receive notifications about the release of
TOMORROW'S DEAD, sign up for Corinna Turner's (occasional)
newsletter at:
www.YandT.co.uk

Aid to the Church in Need

Aid to the Church in Need supports Christians wherever they are persecuted, oppressed or in pastoral need. Founded on Christmas Day 1947 ACN became a Pontifical Foundation of the Catholic Church in 2012. Every year the charity responds to more than 5,000 requests for aid from bishops and religious superiors in around 140 countries, including Syria, Iraq, China, Pakistan, Eritrea and Nigeria. ACN helps bring Christ to the world:

- Seminarians are trained
- Bibles and religious literature are printed
- Priests and religious are supported
- Refugees are helped
- Churches and chapels are built and restored
- More than 50 million Child's Bibles have been printed, in 176 languages
- Religious programmes are broadcast

For regular updates from the suffering Church around the world and to view our full range of books, cards, gifts and music, please log on to our website **www.acnuk.org**

Thank you for helping to dry the tears of the abandoned Jesus on the crosses of this century.
Fr Werenfried van Straaten, O. Praem, founder of *Aid to the Church in Need*

ABOUT THE AUTHOR

Corinna Turner has been writing since she was fourteen and likes strong protagonists with plenty of integrity. She has an MA in English from Oxford University, but has foolishly gone on to work with both children and animals! Juggling work with the disabled and being a midwife to sheep, she spends as much time as she can in a little hut at the bottom of the garden, writing.

She is a Catholic Christian with roots in the Methodist and Anglican churches. A keen cinema-goer, she lives in the UK with her Giant African Land Snail, Peter, who has a six-and-a-half-inch long shell and an even larger foot!

Get in touch with Corinna (and Peter!)...

Facebook/Google+: Corinna Turner

Twitter: @CorinnaTAuthor

Or to receive news and exclusive content, sign up for a (very occasional) newsletter at: *www.YandT.co.uk*

DOWNLOAD YOUR EBOOK

If you own a paperback of *Someday* you can download a free copy of the eBook.

1. Go to *www.YandT.co.uk*
   or scan the QR code:

2. Enter this code on the book's page:
   TXS219G

3. Enjoy your download!

GLOSSARY

Abbu—'Dad'

Allahu akbar—Arabic, 'God is Great'

Ammi—'Mum'

Ayah—a verse from the Quran.

Bride price—An amount of money, property or other form of wealth paid by a groom or his family to the parents of the woman he is to marry.

Bricks and mortar—traveller expression for people who live in permanent houses.

Chichi—Japanese, 'Dad'

CO—Commanding Officer

CU—Christian Union

Dean of Admissions—University official who decides who gets a place.

Dua—Arabic name for informal Muslim prayer/personal supplication (as opposed to formal ritual prayer).

Fish dive—ballet move in which the male dancer supports the female in a 'poisson' (fish) position.

Gakugyō-jōju—*Omamori* with a specific focus on education and passing examinations.

Haha—Japanese, 'Mum'

Hijab—Usually refers to a veil that covers the head and chest, which is worn by some Muslim women beyond the age of puberty in the presence of adult males outside of their immediate family.

Iie—Japanese, 'no'

Insha'Allah—'God willing' or 'If Allah wills'

Kamis—The spirits or phenomena that are worshiped in the religion of Shinto. They are elements in nature, animals, creationary forces in the universe, as well as spirits of the revered deceased.

MOD—Ministry of Defence

Muslimah—A female Muslim

Niqab—Face veil that leaves only the eyes uncovered.

Omamoris—Japanese amulets (charms, talismans) dedicated

to particular Shinto deities and believed to provide various forms of luck or protection.

OTC—Officer Training Corps

R.E.—Religious Education

Shahada—Islamic declaration of faith

Shirk—in Islam, the sin of idolatry or associating beings or things with Allah.

Wali—A custodian or guardian. In Islamic law, a woman needs a *wali* to get married, as the marriage contract is signed by her *wali* and the bridegroom.

Printed in Great Britain
by Amazon